Regina's Surrender

Natasha Perry

For every lover of erotic romance

CHAPTER ONE

Groveland Police Department
Groveland, Illinois

Just when Officer Regina Arrigoni's life had grown downright predictable and stale as day-old bread, her ex-partner entered to rile things up.

She stood in Police Chief Maria Sanchez's doorway, studying Hunter Monroe, where he slouched in a chair beside the chief's desk, his face in profile—until he turned and met Regina's eyes, then slowly rose to his feet.

He was still handsome as a GQ model, but with a few rough edges to him. With his rich brown hair, he always seemed to sport a five o'clock beard by noon, and his eyes were dark and riveting still.

Regina's boss sat behind her desk, dressed in her police-issued navy-blue suit and crisp white shirt, her long indigo-colored hair pinned up neatly as usual. "Have a seat, Officer Arrigoni," she said, indicating with a pen at a chair next to Hunter's. "I believe you two know each other."

What an understatement.

Regina closed the door, paused beside Hunter and shook his

outstretched hand before easing into the chair next to him, bumping elbows with him after he sat down again. The three of them were in a half-circle, almost in a huddle. Memories flooded her mind and soul as she caught his scent, a combination of leather, tobacco and sweat. "Hey, how are you doing?" she softly inquired, turning her body to face him, devouring all of him with a smile on her lips.

He gave her a hard, narrow-eyed look. "Not bad. You?" he asked.

From his body language—how he sat facing the chief and not her spoke volumes. She'd caught a hint of indifference in his tone, but said breezily, "Just hunky-dory."

From his aloof tone, she guessed he held a grudge. Against her. She imagined he was still angry she'd left the force and him two years ago, without telling him. Once he had been released from the hospital and returned home, to his wife, the best thing she could do for herself and him back then was leave Chicago. Closing him out of her life had been the right thing to do.

He'd been the first married man she'd fallen in love with— and the last. Never again. Thank God he never knew about her feelings for him.

"So, long time no see," she said, breaking the silence, guessing he'd say something about her leaving the Chicago police force sooner than later. "What's going on?"

"I'm hoping you can help me work a case."

His lips were turned up into a smirk-style smile that had both irked and excited her in the past. He was still cocky—confident is what *he'd* say. She faced the fact she still adored him. Besides, 'the attitude' suited him.

"This is the job I briefly mentioned yesterday," Chief Sanchez said. Her boss was confident, built like a racehorse, tall and lean —young to be a police chief, at thirty. She was also single, and decidedly a career woman. Never had there been a word of gossip about the chief, though a few of the male officers insinuated she was a lesbian—it was never mentioned aloud. Regina thought, *more power to her.*

The chief rose from her chair, her posture straight and tall.

2

She swung her hips as her long-legged strides carried her to the door. She paused before leaving and added, with a wry smile at them, "I'll leave you two to your discussion. Good seeing you, Hunter."

Hunter inclined his head and the chief left.

Regina knew the case involved the disappearance of a wealthy young woman in Chicago, but that was the extent of information she'd received.

During the years she and Hunter had worked together, Regina had gotten into more than one sticky predicament in the line of duty, in particular the last incident to which they'd responded to, as partners. Never would she forget the gut-wrenching feeling of dread when she saw Hunter take two bullets, in the back. She recalled how her voice trembled as she called in the code for back-up assistance, hovering over him, gun out, watching covertly for his assailant's return.

Once Regina learned Hunter would recover, she'd put in her notice at Chicago Police Department and took her current job in Groveland, a small community not thirty minutes away from her previous station.

Hunter, after healing, remained in Chicago, but had left the force, and had started his own P. I. business, which was now highly successful as Regina had read plenty about him in the newspapers.

After the door closed, Regina turned sideways to face him. "Okay, let's hear it."

He relaxed against the back of his chair with a nod. "The job involves infiltrating a church called The House of Christian Love, though I've several sources who've confirmed it isn't a church at all, but a cover for a sex establishment. It's located smack in the middle of Chicago, near our old beat."

"How long has the woman been missing?"

"About a month."

"The trail's likely gone cold by now," Regina said, stunned.

Hunter grimaced as he crossed one knee over the other. "I don't like it any better than you. Chicago police have been working on it around the clock, from the moment the woman's parents reported her missing, the day after she disappeared. They just recently managed to get someone inside the place."

"That's good. Can they secure a search warrant?"

He shook his head. "Nope. That's why they hired me."

"So, why contact our police department?" she asked.

"The family's originally from Groveland and has donated generously to your mayor's upcoming race. The mayor called and asked your chief for help. Since the case is out of Groveland's jurisdiction, the force can't be directly involved, but your boss suggested, since we knew each other, and had worked together successfully in the past, that you might be willing to help out."

"Darn," she said, under her breath, "I haven't heard a thing about this. Nothing on the news, internet or in the newspapers."

"It's not gone public yet. The woman's father wants it kept quiet, and being a wealthy man helps."

Funny how things always seemed to boil down to either money or politics, or both.

"So, you're saying you've tracked this woman down to this place, right?" At his curt nod, she added, "Tell me what you know so far about this church."

"It's a place that follows the tenets of domestic discipline, though the fact isn't widely known. Most people just know it as one of those strange, cult-like churches."

"Domestic…what?" she said, unable to keep the squeak out of her voice.

Hunter's cool, dark-eyed gaze slid over her curves before finally settling on her eyes.

She cringed, wishing she'd done a better job laying off the donuts since he'd seen her last.

"It's when a wife gives her husband carte blanche over her person. She gives him complete control of their lives, makes all the decisions, basically he's head of household."

A shot of desire blazed through Regina at the look he gave her. It took her a moment to realize he was waiting for a response. "Huh?"

Now the look he leveled on her was impatient and annoyed. Better, she decided.

"Bottom line is, no pun intended, a husband can—discipline his wife if she doesn't do what he says."

"Discipline her?"

"You know what I mean," he snapped as he dropped his crossed leg to the floor.

She shrugged. "No idea what you're talking about, and—"

"You always understood better by doing rather than words," he growled.

She emitted a shriek when he launched her easily over his knee.

"Hunter!" She flailed without success to get up. His arm was an iron band around her waist, holding her in place.

At that moment, the chief stuck her head inside, her eyes wide at first, then narrowed as a small smile slid across her lips. "Sorry. From the noise I thought you were done. I'll just use a phone in another office," she said, then quickly shut the door.

Just as quickly, Hunter yanked Regina back up and pushed her down in her chair again. "You get the idea?"

Regina scowled. "I can't believe this," then added, "does it work both ways?"

Hunter's eyebrows shot up. "What do you mean?"

"Does the wife get to smack the hubby around?"

"Get real, Regina," he drawled, his voice laced with irony.

"This isn't a joke, is it?" She narrowed her eyes on him.

"No. Here's the latest on the case. My client's daughter had been seen entering the place with a man they didn't recognize and hasn't been seen leaving the place since. There just happened to be outdoor cameras outside the facility that caught her. Her family believes she's being detained there against her will. And a steady stream of money has been leaving a joint account the woman has with her parents, funds payable to the House. I could use your back up and experience to get her out of there."

"You mean assuming she's there against her will," Regina replied. At Hunter's nod, she added, "How? What would I need to do?"

"Since we haven't been able to get a search warrant, thought we'd go in undercover with you as my wife."

Wife! Regina gulped, concealing the longing in her heart and, hopefully, her face devoid of expression. How often had she wondered what it would be like being his wife?

"To infiltrate the house, we'd pose as a loving couple—you the dutiful wife wanting to make me, your new husband, completely happy."

"But what exactly does the job entail?"

"Like I said, we'd pose as husband and wife, seeking to live in joyful, marital harmony, in the domestic discipline lifestyle that this particular house upholds. We'd go through training sessions together, rather, you would go through the training. I'd be your trainer, first here, before we enter the house, then we'll receive further instruction upon entering the place."

"Uh-huh." Regina grimaced, beginning to see the nature of the job. She'd had no experience in the area but had heard a bit about the BDSM lifestyle from other cops who had. Dare she go any further with her burning questions? She looked away, thinking how little information she had to make a decision. All she knew was this job, according to her boss, could be her break-out case to advancing her career, which was a huge enticement.

If she made detective, there'd be no more wearing uniforms that fit too snug over her curves and stuck to her in sweltering heat on a day like today. No more talking to school-aged kids about safety and not using drugs but, best of all, no more driving a patrol car aimlessly about the town, waiting for someone to commit a crime; for that matter, waiting for *anything* to happen.

She had only herself to blame for her boring existence. It had been what she thought she'd wanted two years ago. She had applied for and bagged the job as a suburban cop in this wealthy community northeast of Chicago, about half an hour away. In hindsight, she should have stayed with the Chicago force but back then, she'd been sick and tired of big-city street action after Hunter had been shot. She also left, knowing she couldn't trust herself around him any longer. It was months later she learned he'd left the force too.

Back then, Regina and Hunter had been partners. At thirty-four he was seven years older than her, he had always taken the lead and she had always followed, though she had questioned him plenty. Consequently, they'd butted heads on a daily basis, with her generally the loser. She sighed. No matter what anyone said, it was still a 'man's world.' But then, she never minded losing to Hunter since his instincts were keener than hers and, in the end, he was generally right.

Her gaze riveted on him again. His jaw was still angular, his cheekbones high and lips finely chiseled. His deep brown hair, once cut military short, had grown, bangs rakishly long. He gave her a steady look with dark eyes that pierced her body and soul. Heat poured through her, though the air-conditioning was running full blast. He emanated a masculinity that excited her, but she had always concealed her feelings from him. Two years ago, she'd been half-crazy in love with him—but not any longer. *Liar!*

"Regina?" Hunter said, "We need to begin working together on this case sooner than later."

"I'm not sure... I'm thinking this over."

She paused when he rose from his chair, his eyes flickering over her body again, his hands buried in his pants pockets, leaving his jacket open where she could view his package. Quickly, she looked away as heat filled her face.

He shrugged. "Guess it was worth a shot. You wouldn't have been right for the job, anyway."

Inside, Regina bristled, not too surprised he seemed to be taking her uncertainty personally. They had plenty of close, personal history between them; she'd saved his life. You can't get more personal than that.

"I'll find someone else." He turned on his heel, ready to head for the door.

Thinking again about the possibility of advancing in the force, Regina came to a decision and rose from her chair. She couldn't allow this opportunity to slip away. This might be her only chance for promotion for a long while, if ever.

Before he got too far, she stepped after him and clamped a hand around his forearm, feeling his strength.

"Wait a darned minute, Monroe. I need to hear details about this job before I make my final decision."

He chuckled.

She tilted her head back and scowled at him. "Something funny?"

"You're the only cop I've ever heard, male or female, say darn instead of damn." His eyes riveted on her, and he added softly, "Always liked that about you."

She shrugged. "I know of more effective ways to deal with situations than swearing." Not to mention the fact that she'd grown up hearing her father curse, to her mother's everlasting annoyance, yet he'd been a kind, gentle father—also a cop. Neither of her parents had wanted her to become a cop, but nothing they said could deter her. Her father had retired early from the force, though, for her mother's sake. Every time the poor man left to go to work her mother complained and whined for him to find another job. He luckily had come into an unexpected inheritance at the age of forty-three. That was three years ago, and he and her mother spent the cold weather months in Florida, and the rest in Chicago, in the home Regina had grown up in. Now her mother, whenever she spoke to her, asked *her* to find a different line of work, but Regina couldn't. Being a cop was in her blood.

"Yeah, I know." He took her hands, looked down at them with a wry smile. "You bite your nails to the quick, instead."

She shrugged. "So I save money on no manicures."

At his touch, more heat tore through her body and her hands numbed. She put it down to the fact he held her wrists in a tight grip, short-circuiting her circulation. She knew it was an excuse. This man alone had the ability to cause her to feel like a cat in heat, merely from the simple touch of his hand.

While working with him, she'd kept as much distance as possible between them, for good reason; the few times they'd made physical contact all sorts of crazy things had happened to her body—like moisture seeping into every crevice and between her thighs. The man had always affected her that way, but she'd kept her paws off him. In *her* book of ethics, married men were off-limits.

He was still trim and fit. His broad shoulders were clad in a washed linen-look shirt, a solid dark blue tie around his neck. His hips were narrow, and she recalled how fine his ass looked tucked into his uniform pants, or in a pair of jeans. Now he wore a pair of twill slacks, giving him a professional appearance. He looked good, and all of the passion she'd felt in the past crashed to the surface. *Damn!* And now he had her swearing besides, though she decided it didn't count because she did it inside her head.

"I require details, like I said, lots of 'em." She yanked her hands from his, crossed the room, and plopped down on a window ledge.

Hunter raised his brows and folded his arms across his chest. "If we're to keep our cover, you would have to follow every order I give, each and every one, without hesitation, and without argument."

She caught the gleam in his eyes and lifted her chin. "I'm good at following orders, you know that."

"Right," he said skeptically. "Like I said, we'll be pretending we've just returned from our honeymoon. You will need to act as if you're unequivocally surrendering yourself to me."

Surrendering? Regina squirmed at the word yet managed to say, "When we worked together before, you knew you could depend on me."

She saw the sincerity in his eyes and the softening as well. "I can't think of a better cop to cover my back than you. Bottom line, though, we need to convince people we're in love, and that every command I give you will follow."

Regina caught the low purr in his voice, saw how his gaze swept over her body with an intimacy she'd never seen from him before. Something was different about him. Was it her imagination or was he looking at her differently? Like—way differently! With blatant desire, she decided, gazing into his brown orbs again. *Gulp.* "I don't know if I can do that—and be convincing."

"I think you can, or I wouldn't be here. You did when we

were partners, albeit, not without an argument first, but that won't be allowed."

They'd rarely agreed on procedure; he went strictly by the book while she was somewhat of a renegade. Their association, for the most part, had been an emulsion of oil and water for the good times; gasoline on an open flame for the others. They had found a way to live with it. But the most important thing was that they'd always had each other's backs.

He drew near and stopped in front of her. Then her heart sped up when his fingers quickly pulled one strand of her upswept hair loose and he curled it around his finger.

She looked up at him, her mouth gaping, as he examined her hair and spoke softly. "We'll need to spend time together first, practice our relationship so that it's believable, in order to allay any suspicions once we do enter this church, so to speak. There you will pretend to take instruction in how to become the perfect, obedient little spouse."

'Little' had never been a word used to describe Regina. She was five-eight, one-hundred fifty pounds. She scoffed, "Sounds like we're talking about me training to become a Stepford wife."

"That's about it. You're on day shift this week, right?"

She nodded.

"Good. After work each day, we'll work on our roles over the next several days. That should give us enough time to learn our parts."

Sweat gathered on her brow and upper lip at the idea of spending so much time with him. *What am I thinking?* Even play-acting wouldn't work. He was married. She imagined the look on his wife's face when she learned about the job.

Regina shook her head. "There's no way I can be submissive to you, or to any man for that matter."

Hunter scowled, stepped back from her, folding his arms across his chest. "We're talking make believe. Make up your mind. I haven't got time for this."

"The more I hear about this case the less I want to be a part of it. Forget it." She rose from the window's ledge, took a step, and stopped. Hunter had moved into her path.

Reaching out he grasped her shoulders and peered into her eyes. "Why? Be straight with me. We worked together for a few years just fine, and I think we know each other well enough that this shouldn't be too uncomfortable, maybe initially, but we'll get used to each other. And we'll just have to keep reminding ourselves it's a job."

"All right. If I were your wife, I wouldn't want you to do this job with me, that's why."

He frowned. "Sheila and I got divorced a year and a half ago. I assumed you knew."

"I...I had no idea." *It didn't change things. Right!* She stepped out of his hold. "I just can't do the subservient little woman routine. Folks would know we weren't the real thing." She gave him a sardonic once-over. "Besides, we're close to the same size for God's sake." She swept a hand down her body and added, "No one would ever believe you could handle me."

His eyes narrowed. "Are you saying I'm not capable of taking you down?" he snapped.

She nodded, comparing his tall, lean, muscular build against her own. "You got that right. You've got maybe four inches on me, but that's it, and maybe fifty pounds."

His eyes spit fire at her. "You got a gym around here?" he asked.

"Sure do."

His eyes were hot and demanding...not with anger, she decided, but...lust? *No way!*

"Meet me there tonight when you're done with your shift and we'll settle this."

She gulped, prayed he didn't see it, then plastered on an innocent smile. "You're on, Monroe. Six o'clock okay with you?"

"Fine."

"Jackson's Gym is on Fourth Street and Tenth Avenue in the middle of town. You can't miss it."

He nodded. "Let's set the ground rules. When *I* win, you'll do the job, and you'll do it well and follow every order from me. Not to mention the promotion in your department you'll be awarded. Got it?"

Regina loved a challenge same as he, possibly more. And she loved the bantering between them—had missed it.

"When *you* win? You're on, Mister P.I. The way I see it, you've more to gain from all of this than me. What do I get when *I* win, aside from a promotion?"

He rolled his eyes, hands on his hips. "We'd have to keep this on the Q. T. but how much do you owe on your Visa these days?"

Obviously, he remembered how money-management had been a low priority in her life.

She gave him a smug smile and leaned back against the desk. "I have two cards now, a Visa *and* a MasterCard, totaling three k."

He growled and went nose to nose with her. "You deserve a trip over my knee, woman."

Heat flooded her face, and she gawked at him, unable to think of a reply to his audacious comment. Also, she didn't like the wicked gleam in his eyes. More than once, propriety, the nature of their being co-workers, and the fact he was married, had prevented either of them from forming any intimate ties. She had dreamed of him kissing her—dreamed of making love with him—even some kinky stuff…but not a—she could hardly think the word let alone say it—spanking! Discipline. He wouldn't dare.

"Well, have we a deal?" she asked, raising her eyebrows.

"I'll pay them off if you win," he grumbled, "but not before taking my palm to your ass," he warned. "That's part of the deal, got it?"

She gulped and reluctantly nodded. "Deal," she said softly, as she imagined him taking her over his knee. Maybe that kind of kinky stuff wouldn't be too bad… She shook her head. *What in the hell was she thinking?*

"Well, that doesn't sound like much of a win for me, though," she griped.

He remained silent with a smirk on his face. She gulped at the very picture he portrayed and squirmed as she thought about it, biting her bottom lip, looking up at him from beneath her lashes, arms folded behind her, hands resting on her seat pants pockets. There was no way he'd do it, she decided, then grinned.

"You're on, Monroe," adding, "I like the idea of being debt-free." *But at the price of a humiliating experience culminating in a sore ass if he won the match? Nah, he wouldn't do it.*

CHAPTER TWO

Regina worked out religiously. She had the kind of body that turned to flab if she didn't. Also, it didn't help that she was a carbo-holic, but the martial arts training and workouts raised her metabolic rate, which kept off the weight, and her three days a week weight training kept her strong and solid. Genetics played a huge part in her build; she had the plump ass and full tits of her Italian mother. No changing that, she knew, unless she underwent surgery, which she wouldn't do.

Feeling not as confident as she had when accepting the challenge that she could kick Hunter's arrogant ass, she arrived at the gym fifteen minutes early to find him already there, laughing and talking with some of her cop-cohorts. Dressed head to toe in black sweatpants and t-shirt, and barefoot, he looked amazing.

As she watched the antics of her fellow cops she thought, good grief, what was it about male camaraderie that made her blood boil? She knew the answer, even though she hated to admit it; she'd never had any close male or female friends. She'd been painfully shy as a child, preventing her from making any truly meaningful friendships. And when her height shot up so she towered over all of the other girls in her sixth grade class, her introversion worsened. It had taken her years to emotionally grow into her tall frame. The closest friend she'd ever had, ironically, was Hunter.

Hunter met up with her outside the ring, his sultry gaze sliding over her appreciatively. She wore a sweater over her standard workout uniform; black low-slung capri sweats with a black sports bra. Removing her sweater, she dropped it over a chair.

"You can back out now, if you like," he offered.

"Not a chance. Let's get going. I've got a date tonight," she lied.

As she climbed over the ropes and entered the ring, Hunter followed her. "Oh, yeah? Glad to see you've finally got a social life."

Regina glared at him over her shoulder, saw his eyes were on her ass before he could slide them up to meet her eyes. She slid off her sandals and started dancing on her toes, facing him. He knew her too well. To anyone else, Hunter would appear a threat, but not to her; she knew he'd give her a good workout but would never harm her. They'd agreed on the method of fighting. She would use her martial arts training while he would use the standard self-defense he'd learned in police academy. Now, as she took in his devilishly good looks, she decided only Hunter could look *this* good in a pair of ordinary sweats, t-shirt, and barefoot.

The owner of the gym, Ron Jackson, stepped up and stated the rules. Whomever took down the other three times to the mat first was the winner. And by down, it meant entire body down, not just to knees. Hunter outweighed her, increasing his chances, but she knew the moves—knew *his* moves. She had just as good a chance of taking him down.

They started trading strikes with the heels of their hands. She delivered several hard kicks with the sides of her feet, keeping the blows low per the rules dictating fair fighting.

To her chagrin, they'd drawn a crowd, most of them her fellow cops, cheering them on—correction—a few voices encouraged her, but the lion's share egged him on. She wasn't surprised. Hadn't it always been the boys against the girls?

Usually, Regina was slow to anger, but had reached her limit when she heard someone call out shortly after they'd started, "Come on! She's a girl for cryin' out loud. Take her down!"

Hunter turned away when she struck out with a side kick,

missing him, but then, unfortunately, his taut, finely sculpted ass in his sweats distracted her. Damn, she'd forgotten how his build had always been a distraction and he took advantage as he charged her coming out of a circle, swept a leg behind hers causing her to lose her balance and fall to the mat.

As she lay on her back, she sighed, looking up at the shit-eating grin on his face. "One down," she whispered, "but not one more."

"Riiight," he drawled.

The next down was hers when she tripped him up and he landed hard on his back. She pounced on top of him, her hands holding his down on the mat on either side of his head. Now it was her turn to grin. "Tied."

He clasped her hands, pressed up raising her, then pulled them toward him and tossed her over his head. She rolled over him and landed on her back but couldn't get up quick enough. He pinned her down.

"Two," he breathed, his eyes darkening as they swept across her face.

Regina felt the heat of his body as he sat on her stomach, his eyes taking in her breasts before he scrambled to his feet, took her wrist and pulled her up then danced away from her.

On her feet once more she positioned herself in a crouched stance. It didn't really matter if she won or not because she planned on doing the job, the temptation to work with Hunter too much of an enticement for her to ignore. She also knew she didn't have much of a chance of putting him down twice more, but she wasn't giving up.

She started to deliver a sharp side kick to his knee when she slipped. Catching herself when she started to fall, a hand touched the floor and the blow from her foot landed too high, striking Hunter, who'd turned away, but not in time. She hit him in the kidney.

Hunter arched back and clutched his lower back, grimacing. "Fuck," he gasped.

Regina groaned when she realized the inaccuracy of her strike, the spectators' condemning murmurs screaming in her ears. Vital organs were off-limits. She felt awful. Never would she intention-ally harm him. Stepping back, she gave him room to recover, her hands jammed on her hips as she apologized. "Sorry. It was an accident. I slipped."

The men standing around the ring wore chagrinned expres-sions. Fellow cop, Jerry O'Malley, thankfully said, "We saw you, Regina. It *was* an accident." They turned away, returning to their own exercise regimes.

Tentatively, she touched his shoulder and whispered, "Are you okay?"

At his nod she turned away, quickly headed for the door, guessing he'd want nothing to do with her after this—accident or not.

She heard pounding steps come up behind her. She started to turn when a pair of big hands suddenly clamped around her waist and spun her in a circle. Regina yelped, caught just a momentary glimpse of Hunter's taut expression before he hoisted her up and over his shoulder, and her body flopped over his back.

She was too stunned to do anything as he strode from the gym. He'd positioned one arm over her thighs below her ass, keeping her anchored as raucous cheers echoed in their wake.

She came to her senses and started pounding on his back as they neared the door. "You cheater, you were faking all along!"

"No, I wasn't. I hurt like hell," he snarled. "You've got a lesson coming, and I'm pissed off enough to give it to you, accident or not." He picked his way carefully across the parking lot, cursing, "Damn, I left our shoes back there and now my feet are killing me."

"Serves you right!"

She pushed against his shoulders, straightening up, kicking her legs when he paused in his stride and landed one swat on her ass. She yelped.

"Hold still," he growled.

Shrieking in protest, she started kicking more, but escape was useless. He had a death-grip on her.

"Your pals will gather our stuff and put it in a locker. I'll come back later and retrieve it all."

She grabbed a swatch of his hair and yanked on it. He came to a dead stop, pushed her further up over his shoulder and said, "You want another smack?"

"No," she grumbled and stopped kicking. "I said I'd do the job if you won, didn't I?" she bellowed.

"Oh, there's no doubt in my mind you'll do it." He reached his car, opened the passenger door, and dumped her inside.

She moaned before twisting and sticking her feet out the open door. He blocked her exit and glared at her, his legs spread to block her, hands on his hips. "Don't even think about it."

She gave him a cool, level look. "Okay, what's with the caveman tactics? I can't believe you...you...hit me."

"I spanked you, one tap, and I'll be doing a hell of a lot more to you than that during this job, Regina."

Then she heard him cursing under his breath.

"Temper, temper," she said, somewhat nervous as she thought about his threat—worrying about having to take on the damned job, but he'd won, as she said, by default.

His anger surprised her. She'd always been the one quicker to anger, and it had only been on rare occasion when he'd lost control. She'd never been fearful of him, but now his anger unsettled her. She'd always managed to aggravate him, but he usually reacted in annoyance, not anger.

He stepped back. "Legs inside and snap on the seatbelt."

"What about my car?"

"I'll drive you back later to get it."

She lifted her legs in and faced forward, snapping on her seatbelt as she tried to recall if he'd ever been this bossy before. After some thought she decided he hadn't been. What? Was this new for him then? Was he possibly already 'acting' the part of dominant husband before starting the job? Or has he always been a closet dominant, at least toward her. She always felt he'd treated her like an equal.

Patting the black leather interior of a new Volvo she shot him a curious look. "Your business must be doing well?"

"Damned straight," he said. He slammed her door shut then came around to the driver's side. Planting himself behind the steering wheel, he swiveled to face her and slid his arm along the back of the seat.

He sat in silence for a moment and stared at her. She went still so as not to squirm in her seat, his expression even more unsettling.

CHAPTER THREE

Hunter had always been an ass man, and Regina's ass was premier in his book.

As he stared at her, he tried to figure out a way to tell her what he'd learned about Christian domestic discipline in the stack of e-books he'd managed to secure from online stores catering to that persuasion. He'd also found several from the local library.

From what he knew of *this* particular organization they'd be infiltrating he didn't believe for a minute they were Christian-based. He guessed money was the reason for the organization's existence, having learned the entry fee alone was $15,000.

In order to maintain credibility that he and Regina were happy newlyweds looking to set their marriage in the right direction, Regina would have to put on a damned good act—as would he. But it wouldn't be difficult—for him.

Mostly, the literature talked about punishment and maintenance spankings used for correction, and denial of orgasms—for the woman, not the man, of course, he mused dryly.

In the past, he'd delved plenty into alternative lifestyles undercover in his line of work as a police officer, pre-Regina-partner days. The nature of this so-called church they'd be infiltrating wasn't completely foreign to him as he'd also participated in the 'scene' himself. And since he and his wife parted ways, he'd become a member of an exclusive club in Chicago. He'd enjoyed participating in scenes with various submissives, though none had been permanent in his life. He'd never taken a submissive for his own and didn't plan to in the future.

Suddenly, the thought of Regina being his submissive seemed right—natural to him. Though she doubted herself, he didn't. He could well imagine her in the role.

He guessed that Regina had never been exposed to this type of work, though; had never gone to a BDSM club before and thought it pertinent to ask her sooner than later. *Damn.* Then he thought how well did he know her? Sure, they'd been partners, but hell, he couldn't remember her ever even having a stable, romantic relationship. She'd turned twenty-seven on her last birthday, and he found it difficult to believe she hadn't had some experience with men. He was counting on her having had a little, at the least. His lip quirked into a small smile as he thought about 'taking her in hand' as the books mentioned.

Knowing Regina, he guessed she would protest, even if they would be acting, still she wouldn't have a choice. It was imperative she accept his dominant role, at least until they'd gained the information he needed regarding his client's daughter.

Her muttered words caught his attention. "I apologize, Hunter. You won fair and square. Sorry about that kick. Like I said, I slipped."

After a tense, silent moment, he sighed. "I know it was an accident, and I admit I should have found another way to encourage you to take the job without making you feel so defensive."

"Yes, you should have," she retorted.

"Well, how the hell do you think I felt when you insinuated you could clean up the floor with me?"

His heart lurched at the quick, sunny grin crossing her face. "You shouldn't have challenged me."

Hunter hooked her neck with one arm and dragged her close. Her softness and scent hit him hard and he tightened his arm around her, pulling her against him—as close as he could with the gearshift in his way. Her eyes widened on him and her body stiffened. Nearly on the edge of releasing her, she surprised him when she wound both arms around his neck and kissed him, right smack on the lips.

His hands started swarming over every inch of her body, fingers sliding over her breasts, cupping them through the bra's stretchy fabric, then moving lower to her waist. She was built the way he liked his women; full breasted, flaring hips, full, curvy ass, narrow waist, and mile-long legs. Oh yeah, legs that would easily wind around him when they had sex.

A voice inside him warned, *This is Regina, not just any woman.* But he couldn't resist sliding his hand even lower, to her thighs, between them where he rubbed her hot center through her cropped sweatpants.

She moaned and leaned into him. Good. She accepted his touch. Maybe this job would be easier than he thought it would be. Damn, he didn't want to think of this, of them together in a job, but together, physically, and emotionally, for real. Until now, he hadn't realized how much he'd missed her. He stroked, nibbled, and kissed her with a firm yet gentle touch, his one hand still planted between her thighs, until he heard her whispering frantically and pressing against his shoulders.

"Stop, Hunter."

Reluctantly he released her with a scowl. "This will be the last time. If you didn't want this to go anywhere, why'd you kiss me?"

Settling back in his seat he watched her fold her hands protectively across her chest, moving up and down with her agitated breathing. Damn it, he should know better. He was older and wiser.

"I couldn't help myself. Dang," she muttered, "where in the hell did *that* come from?"

Apparently, he wasn't the only one surprised by their shared kisses and growing need. He got a grip on his raging hormones, told himself this was a job and that he couldn't afford to take it personally. "Call it practice for things to come."

"So, you didn't mean that kiss?"

"It means that's one of the gentler things I'll do to you on a daily basis once we begin practicing in order to infiltrate the House of Christian Love."

Regina lifted one arched eyebrow and asked breathily, "What else?"

Hunter sighed. "I'll explain later, which is why I asked if you could act. What I'll be asking of you won't be at all…well… natural to you, or easy."

She scowled and planted her back against the passenger door again. "We have to talk."

"No kidding," he said dryly as he turned the key in the ignition. He stared down at his feet. "I can't remember the last time I drove without shoes."

"Hmm, I think it was that one stake-out we did at Parson's Funeral Home."

"Yeah, I think you're right. Where can we go to get comfortable?"

"My place." She glanced at her watch. "It's five o'clock and I'm starved. I'll cook us supper."

Hunter grinned, liking the sound of food and us. He also knew Regina was a damned fine cook. "Uh, any chance you've got some of that homemade pasta sauce you always used to make?"

"As a matter of fact, I do. I'll thaw it in the microwave, and we'll have spaghetti."

Hunter leaned over and kissed her again, right on her plump lips.

She raised her brow. "You must be hungry."

Oh, yeah, but not for just your sauce. "You know I can't resist your spaghetti and meatballs."

"Did I say anything about meatballs?"

"You always have meatballs with your sauce." He knew her well.

As he drove, he started thinking about while he'd been her partner, he'd never felt any sexual stirrings for her. But then, he had been a happily married man and true to his vows and his love for his wife. But life with Sheila had changed when she became a born-again Christian, after the death of their three-month old son to SIDS. The marriage ended when she didn't turn to him for comfort, or give it in return, but had turned to her new faith instead. And she'd also kicked him out of their bed, with the excuse of not wanting to get pregnant again. No man could live that way for the rest of his life. She didn't want him.

It had taken him months to get over his love for her. To this day, he still felt twinges of it. He harbored resentment about her choice in life, which was one of the reasons why he had been so quick to take on this job. He guessed this was just another cult built on false beliefs in order to make money, the price to be paid by stupid, unsuspecting women accompanied by unscrupulous men. He knew that some of the women at the house were not married to their guys—not a requirement—marriage, but learning submission was.

Hunter drove as Regina gave him directions to her house. Soon he pulled into her driveway. He'd never seen her place before. He shut off the car and took in the gardens on either side of the walkway lush with color, smiling when he looked at the monstrous Victorian home. "Interesting color," he said.

"Isn't it?" she said with glee. "I painted it myself."

She'd painted the house purple—yep—purple, the trim a creamy white with a tint of…was that pink? Hunter tried to couch his response so that she wouldn't take offense. He said, "It's unusual."

She frowned. "You hate it."

"To tell you the truth, I didn't know anyone made purple exterior paint. Somehow, you don't seem like the type that would paint your house such a girlie color."

"It's orchid, not purple. Are you insinuating I'm butch?"

"Got it. Orchid." Leveling a hard look at her when she jammed her hand on the door latch, he said, "Stay put."

He came around and opened her door, ignoring her last question, knowing she was sensitive about her size, recalling how self-conscious she'd been, especially when his ex would try and set her up with dates. He frowned and thought how he'd only known her to have had a few dates in the past. He knew she spent most of her time at home, working, or spending time with her huge

Italian family in Chicago, whom she adored, and he did too, for that matter.

He gingerly followed her past the garden beds and up the stairs leading to her front door. She opened the door, started to kick off her shoes, then stopped, obviously remembering she wasn't wearing them. Memories flooded Hunter when he recalled her performing the same movement at the station every time she settled down before her computer.

Inside Regina's spacious kitchen, he followed the swing of her hips as she disappeared down a hall, then returned a few minutes later, wearing a black tank top that stopped above her navel.

Hunter's body tightened at the sight of Regina in the form-fitting top, especially since she'd removed the bra and he saw her nubs had gone hard. She had also changed into camouflage colored sweatpants which hung enticingly low on her hips, still barefoot.

She set him to work cutting up tomatoes and cucumbers for a salad while she nuked the sauce she'd pulled from the freezer, then set a pan to boiling on the cooktop for the pasta. He was happy for the diversion.

He sank into a chair at her kitchen table after preparing the salad, his eyes settling on Regina's lushly curved ass as she worked at the counter, her back to him. There was a space of creamy skin between her top's bottom edge, and the waistline of her pants. A hint of a cleft...

She poured water into the coffee maker and set it to brew. Soon the aroma of fresh coffee filled the space. Then he watched her uncork a bottle of merlot and pour them each a glass.

He pulled at the neckline of his sweatshirt and looked away, imagining sliding his hands over her ass and squeezing the full globes.

Half an hour later, Hunter had eaten two heaping helpings of pasta and meatballs before settling back in his chair, rubbing his stomach.

"You'll make some guy a great wife one day." *Like me.* He scowled. Where in the hell had *that* come from.

"Because I can cook?" She rose from her chair, picked up

25

their plates and utensils. At the sink, she rinsed them off and loaded them in the dishwasher. He narrowed his eyes on her ass again, noticing how her pants stretched taut and conformed around it. She turned to face him, and his gaze landed on her eyes before she could see where they'd been. Then she leaned against the sink, a half-smile on her lips.

He grinned back. She'd removed her hair clip, and her mass of auburn-colored tresses fell in loose waves past her shoulders, ending at her lower back, just where her spine curved above her ass. She'd worn her hair just to her shoulders two years ago, so this was a surprising change—her long hair. He tried not to focus on her full breasts jutting out beneath her snug top, even as he thought about how to respond. After a while he murmured, "Yeah, among other things."

She sent him a narrow-eyed look. "What other things."

"Things," he said gruffly before turning to stare out the kitchen window, thinking about their earlier kiss. He mentally kicked himself for the comment.

The window overlooked her back yard, and he admired the manicured bushes, trimmed trees, and more flowers—everywhere. The woman must live outside every moment she could.

She said, "Okay, let's head out to the porch to talk details. Coffee?"

"Sure."

She poured tall cups of coffee for each of them and doused hers with cream. Passing him his cup, she picked up her own and headed for the porch, and he followed. They sank down onto wicker chairs covered in green-striped cushions. Raising their legs, they hooked them over the porch's center railing in perfect synchronization, as though they'd done it a hundred times before.

They sipped their coffee in companionable silence. After a while Hunter cleared his throat and tried to figure out how to proceed when Regina spoke.

"Tell me about your client and how she got involved in this stuff in the first place."

"Does the name Matilda Matthews ring a bell?"

Regina gasped her eyes wide on him. "You mean the heiress?"

He nodded.

"Family's into shipping, oil, and just about anything else that makes money," she said.

Hunter was thankful Regina hadn't barraged him with questions. He saw the distant look in her eyes and knew she was thinking over the situation in her typical street-smart style.

Regina had been raised in a working-class family in inner city Chicago, while he'd been born and raised an only child in an upper-crust suburban area of New York, to parents who'd expected him to take over the family stock brokerage firm. To his parents' disappointment, Hunter had other plans.

"Go on," Regina encouraged.

He focused on her long legs and wondered how she'd look in a short skirt, any skirt, for that matter. Never had he seen her in anything but uniform pants, sweats, and jeans.

"About six months ago, Matilda dropped her approved-by-the-family fiancé and took up with an unknown guy—a tennis instructor she'd met at the country club. She brought the guy home a couple times. Her family had him investigated. They learned he possessed no important lineage and had no money. They hated him and said he wasn't good enough for their daughter. And when they forced the issue, insisting she end the relationship, she took off with him. They hadn't heard from her in a month but had recently learned from one of Matilda's friends that she had planned to marry the guy."

"Do you know for a fact she's at this house?"

"Oh, yeah. There's already a Chicago P.D. police informant working undercover inside I've been told. And as I mentioned, the cameras caught her entering the place."

"By herself?"

He nodded. "Yeah. We think the boyfriend was already there, waiting for her."

"Footage of him?" she asked.

"Surprisingly, no, but the informant says he's there."

She frowned. "Then why isn't the informant intervening?"

"Because he needs to remain undercover for some other stuff happening at the house—a possible drug issue. The house hired him for muscle, under a fictitious cover, so he's there being watchful and careful, and reporting back—but the force hasn't instructed him to do anything else.

"Also, we questioned some of Matilda's friends. Matilda had told them about the house, and that she'd be spending some time there with her soon-to-be husband."

"Location?"

"Like I said, smack in the middle of Chicago. I'm not surprised since these places generally keep a low profile."

"So, what's our next step?"

"I've already set up an interview for us."

"What sort of qualifications would one need to be accepted?"

"Not much, except for money."

"That leaves me out," she said dryly.

"Yes, well, this is one time I'm using my family's reputation and my money. The Matthews family will reimburse me, of course, afterwards."

Regina gasped. "You mean you're going to tell these people that you're the scion to the internationally renowned Monroe Brokerage firm? You're not going to use an alias?"

"That's right."

"Once they check you out won't they be suspicious when they learn you're an ex-cop and now a P.I.?"

"Possibly, but it won't be the first time a cop enlists a cult's services. As long as I sign on the dotted line that I won't take issue with them, after the fact, and turn a blind eye to the goings-on there, they'll accept us and my money. Which won't mean a hell of a lot once we can prove they're breaking the law by keeping the Matthews woman against her will, that piece of paper will be null and void."

"Any reason why we can't just pay them a visit, lay it on the line and ask them outright?"

"Matilda's parents believe she's on the run. If she learns she's being followed she'll run again. They want, at the very least, an opportunity to try and talk her home. Assuming she's a willing participant in all of this, but there is a chance, as I said, that she's being held against her will."

"Isn't Matilda over twenty-one?"

"Twenty-five." Hunter held up his hand. "I know. She's old enough to make her own decisions and her parents don't have a say about it, still, the family's paying me well to find her and, at the minimum, make a report on her welfare, which I intend to do, with your help. Once we're accepted into this house, I want you to get real close to Matilda, take her into your confidence. Listen to her. Find out if she's being treated right, and that she's not there against her will."

Nodding, she asked, "Are we going to force her to leave, even if she's happy there?"

Hunter shook his head. "Already told the parents we can't do it since Matilda is an adult. It's her life, her call. I'll show you her picture, but you likely already know what she looks like."

"Yeah, the family's been in the news often—along with photos. So, that's it?" Regina asked.

"Not quite. We'll have a week to work on your part." He flicked a quick glance over her figure. "You'll need to wear different clothes at the house, feminine stuff but classy."

"Uh, this is about all I have, besides jeans and my uniforms."

He shrugged. "No problem." He dug into his back pocket, pulled out a money clip and peeled off several hundred dollar bills. "Buy a few dresses and skirts, classy but sexy, and some high heels."

She took the money, but said dryly, "You know that I'll be nearly your height with heels."

He shrugged again. "You saw earlier, your height doesn't bother me."

"You're a rare exception," she muttered.

He put his legs down, stood up, and held out his hand.

She took it and he pulled her to her feet. Before she could even think of anything more to say, he drew her close, winding his arms around her waist, until her breasts brushed against his chest. He focused on her lips, started lowering his head but paused when she pulled back a bit.

Heaving a deep sigh, he kept his arms around her and murmured, "Get used to my touch. We'll be getting real close soon and staying that way until we've completed the job to mine and my client's satisfaction. The quicker you learn to be comfortable and intimate with me, the sooner we'll be able to find out the information we need and finish the job."

"But—"

He crushed her lips beneath his, let up some pressure, then stabbed his tongue inside her mouth when he felt her body relax against him. She sucked on his tongue like a lollipop. He felt his lower extremities hardening, his cock thickening, lengthening, seeking her heated core. His hands cupped her ass. He squeezed one globe, felt her body tense up. Reluctantly, he released her, got himself under control, and took two steps back.

He noticed her breathing had quickened and her eyes had that deer in headlights look. Damn, he didn't mean to scare her.

Then, the question that permeated his mind for a long time made him ask, "Why'd you leave the force, Regina?"

She gave him a confused look. "Leave?"

"Yes. Last I saw you was when I woke up in the hospital, then you left without saying a word and never returned. Why? Why give up everything—your years on the force—our working relationship—to come here?"

Hunter noted the pain crossing her face as he waited for her to answer him. He'd wanted to ask her this question for two years, but they hadn't communicated at all once she'd left Chicago. Several times he'd wanted to call her, but the ball was in her court. She was the one who left him.

Tears filled her eyes as she nodded. "Yes, you deserve an answer, and this may cause you to regret asking me to do this job with you."

"No way will I regret that," he said gruffly.

"It was too much for me—seeing you shot—seeing you so close to death in that alley. Me screaming for help into the radio like a freakin' little girl, and back-up taking forever. Believing you would die."

He understood that, thinking how he'd felt when his son had died—and he hadn't had a chance to know him. It had changed his life and his wife's.

Nodding, he muttered, "I'm going to the hotel to get some shuteye. I'll be back around ten in the morning."

"What for?"

"We're going shopping." He caught the high color seeping into her cheeks and smiled.

"I'm working and won't be able to shop until my shift's over."

"You sure are working," he said, a low grin forming on his lips, "with me. Don't worry. I've already talked to your boss and she's approved your absence for all next week, with pay of course."

"I can handle my own shopping." She shoved the money at him. "And I can pay for my own clothes."

He took the money back. "Yeah, right, so you can add more to your credit cards? No way. Now that I think about it, I'll use plastic tomorrow. This cash won't buy all the things I think you'll need."

"I don't want you shopping with me. I'm a big girl."

His grin widened. "Uh-huh, but I'm going. I wouldn't miss *this* transformation for the world."

CHAPTER FOUR

Regina was surprised the following morning when she looked out her living room window and saw her car in her driveway, but no sign of Hunter. He must have driven it over sometime last night, she decided, then walked back to the Marcom Hotel where he was staying.

She finished her light make up routine when she heard the doorbell ring and she answered to find Hunter on her doorstep, exactly on time.

"Hey, thanks for driving my car back. It must have been late last night. And how did you get home then?"

He shrugged. "Figured I'd have a good run back to the hotel."

Yeah, she mused, thinking about the hilly seven miles back to where he was staying. Then she remembered him occasionally waking her up from a deep sleep on her days off work in Chicago, coercing her into running with him—not her favorite sport—still it meant spending leisure time with him so she never turned him down.

She hitched her purse onto her shoulder.

"Got your keys, right?" he asked.

She rolled her eyes and patted her purse. "Yes."

"Just checking," he muttered.

Heat filled her cheeks then as she thought about how, more than a few times back in Chicago, he'd had to break into her apartment because she'd left her keys inside. She groaned then as she thought about the tormenting hours ahead. Initially, she'd dreaded the idea of Hunter assisting her in choosing new appropriate clothing, especially since she figured he'd insist she model them for him, too. But, after some thought, the idea didn't distress her too much. She'd give him an eyeful and she grinned at the thought. He'd said she needed tasteful clothing, but he hadn't given any other criteria.

With a sigh, she stepped outside, forcing Hunter to back down a step.

"I gather you're ready," he said dryly.

She glared at the smirk on his lips. "As ready as I'll ever be. Let's get this over with." She poked his chest. "And no smart-ass comments from you about the clothes I choose, understand? I know what looks good on me and what doesn't."

Hunter's brow lifted. "Really? You don't own a dress, but I think you'd look great in one."

"Take my word that I look better in pants."

"Uh-uh." He backed down to the sidewalk and swept a slow, lingering gaze from her feet to her waist. "With those long legs, you'll look dynamite in a skirt."

She gave an un-lady snort by way of reply.

"Come on." He snagged her arm and escorted her to his car. "You've got some studying to do once we're through shopping so the sooner we finish the better."

"Studying?"

"I'll explain later."

On the road, she kept quiet, staring out the window, ignoring the delicious-looking man beside her. Ironically, they were dressed similarly, almost as though they'd called each other to coordinate! The both wore belted black jeans, her with a red t-shirt while he wore a short-sleeved black t that made him seem even taller and leaner than he already was. Her mouth watered as she glimpsed down at his muscular thighs clad in the perfect fitting jeans. Her face heated when he caught her looking at him and he grinned. Tilting her nose up she turned away and hugged the passenger door.

Within twenty minutes they arrived at Rachel's, an expensive boutique in Groveland's downtown area and Hunter expertly maneuvered his Volvo into a parking spot.

As soon as Regina entered the shop, decorated in cool gray, blue, and cream colors, panic set in. She wasn't used to being, as Hunter put it, a girlie-girl. Her height and full curves had been a problem for her during her teen years, so she'd always downplayed her femininity by dressing in jeans and slacks—never a dress.

She cringed when she thought about the last time she'd worn a skirt. It had been her sophomore year in high school. Paul Anderson, a classmate for whom she'd harbored a major crush had, amazingly, asked her to the prom. Not only was he a handsome, popular guy, he was captain of the football team. He'd also been the only guy in her entire class who towered over her, though that had changed by her senior year when the boys finally caught up in height and beyond with the girls.

Later, in the ladies' room, she'd overheard a humiliating conversation between a couple girls as she sat on the toilet. Paul had made a bet with a couple of guys that he could make 'ice queen', Regina Arrigoni, fall in love with him. Amidst the girls' laughter, they'd made snide remarks about Regina's height and lack of style, including the gaudy dress she'd worn to prom—a pink frothy number her mother had chosen for her.

She'd gotten through the night, avoided Paul's kisses upon arriving at her house after the dance, and ran inside. She never saw him again after that since school ended the week following the prom. After that, she'd dated little in the past ten years. Most men she met that she liked became friends because that's all she'd allow them to be. And she could count on one hand how many men she'd slept with—just a couple guys from police academy.

"Earth to Regina."

Regina glanced up and noted Hunter's quizzical smile.

"Where were you?" he asked, his eyes delving deep into hers.

"Just thinking," she muttered. "Let's get the show on the road."

Rachel's wasn't the type of store where a woman could browse the racks. A sleek, fashionably dressed, narrow-faced saleswoman escorted Hunter and Regina into a private sitting room. While Hunter sank into a lushly upholstered chair, Regina was hustled into a dressing room.

The saleswoman helped Regina remove her clothes, then left to choose several outfits. While stylish clothing had never been important to Regina, underwear was. Now she stood in her last extravagant purchase from Victoria's Secret, a golden-colored lacy bra and matching thong. While her outer clothes were utilitarian, she'd always loved sexy underwear, and indulged herself often. Soon the saleswoman returned. Regina's eyes widened on the dresses she'd draped across her arms, then proceeded to hang them from hooks on the walls.

"Oh, my," Regina breathed, then darted a worried look at the woman. "Help me, please?"

"Of course," the woman said, her trained eye on Regina. "You're a lucky woman. You have the height and figure to carry off any one of these dresses. I'd stay away from ruffles, though lace would look wonderful on you."

Waving her arm at the clothing, Regina asked, "Uh, what do you suggest?"

The woman swept her skilled eyes across the dresses, finally settling on a black sheath, then the other, a teal-blue dress with a fitted, corset-style waistline that laced up the front, the narrow skirt ended well above her knee. Regina donned the teal-colored dress first, which also had narrow, elbow-length sleeves and a low, rounded neckline that displayed her cleavage. Regina gasped, "It's gorgeous but too fancy for everyday wear."

"Your gentleman said you must choose two cocktail dresses, and several other dresses for daytime and skirts and separates for casual wear, um, but no slacks. He said you already own several pair."

The woman convinced Regina to model the dresses for Hunter. With her chin raised, she stood before him. Flashes of heat soared from her feet to her cheeks and she couldn't meet his eyes. She felt Hunter's gaze sweep over every inch of her body, raising his finger and twirling it, indicating she turn. She did a complete swivel around, then faced him before he heartily approved of both dresses.

The saleswoman left to answer the phone.

"Liar."

Regina met his ardent gaze. "Excuse me?"

"You said you look awful in skirts. I beg to differ. You were born to wear them, sweetheart. If you were mine, I'd never allow you to wear pants."

By the time Regina thought of a sarcastic reply to his audacious, arrogant comment, the saleswoman had returned so she kept her mouth shut, glaring at Hunter's cynical expression and twitching lips.

"We'll take this one, and the last one as well." He smiled at Regina. "Try on something else, darling. Perhaps some nice lingerie?" His comment directed at the saleswoman.

Stumbling back to the dressing room, Regina forgot her anger and her mouth watered when the saleswoman followed her in with several delicate but minuscule pieces of underwear. Regina found it quite easy to make her choices. Just as she donned a black Merry Widow and matching thong the telephone rang again.

"Go ahead and try on the other things, my dear," said the saleswoman. "By the way, *that* is exquisite on you." After the woman left, Regina took one more look in the mirror and decided she had to purchase the corset for herself. She glimpsed the price tag, groaned, and thought forget it. She started to unlace the ribbons when she glanced up at the sound of the door opening and Hunter slipping inside, closing the door behind him.

"Get out!" she whispered harshly as with one hand she tried concealing her boobs and the other her vulva.

He leaned against the door, folding his arms across his broad chest. "Since I'm paying, I have the right to look." His lips turned up into a devilish grin. "Now I know why you hadn't come out again. I like what I see, no doubt about it, as for me leaving—no way. You need to get used to me hanging around you, in all states of dress—and undress. And now is as good a time as any to begin training you to become used to me and my touch."

"Not here," she warned.

"Uh-uh." He wagged his finger near her nose. "Not a submissive attitude at all. You-will-learn soon enough what happens when you don't obey me."

His eyes darkened, passion flaring deep inside as he stared at her. "Like I said, I need you to get comfortable with me in both private and public places." He wound his hands around her shoulders and turned her around so that her back was to him. Her eyes widened on the two of them, catching their reflection in the full-length mirror.

He reached around her with both hands, and she watched him loosen the ribbons down the front of the corset. Shivers of desire tore up her spine at the very thought of him seeing her breasts, then self-consciousness filtered through her again.

Opening her mouth to object she saw his warning look and, clamping her teeth together, she stifled her protests.

They both stilled when the saleswoman called out, "Miss? I have another call and will return as soon as I can. Oh, by the way, it seems your gentleman friend slipped out for a bit."

"Oh, I'm afraid—"

His hand covered her mouth.

She nodded and waited until she heard the woman's steps move away from the door. Uncovering her mouth, he grasped her arms and turned her to face him. "This isn't personal, you know. We're acting, that's all, preparing for a job."

Her racing pulse calmed at his reminder and she nodded. *Right. A job.*

"Remember those credit card bills? Oh, and don't forget about the job advancement."

His dangling the carrot again reminded her to cooperate. He turned her to face the mirror again and she waited with anticipation of whatever exquisite torment he had planned for her. She saw how his gaze traveled down the front of her body. His eyes riveted on the tops of her breasts bursting out of the loosened corset bodice. His eyes widened then, and his nostrils flared, his face filled with passion. She guessed what he was thinking. How could this possibly be the same woman he'd partnered with for over two years? She hadn't changed a bit, but then he'd been married and had eyes only for his wife back then.

He finished unlacing the garment then pulled it away, dropping it to the bench beside them. Moving around he paused in front of her, reached out and traced the blue veins across her upper breasts with one finger, then moved lower. He caressed one nipple, then the other.

Regina had closed her eyes, and felt like purring, content as a kitten being stroked by its master. Her breathing quickened as he continued gently stroking her, then cupping both of her breasts in his hands. She arched her back, pushing out her breasts, wishing he'd suckle her nipples.

Disappointment set in when his hands slid away from her breasts and down to her waist. He caressed her stomach, then casually slid one finger inside the front of her thong. Holding her breath until he released her and moved behind her again, to look at her reflection in the mirror.

She felt his hand on her lower back then, pressing down. At first, she wasn't certain what he wanted until he spoke.

"Bend over," he encouraged her, his voice low and sultry.

She stiffened at his order, but then stepped back from the wall to take the position, bumping into his chest until he backed up also. Then growing arousal and heat coursed through her body, and she felt heat seep into her face, embarrassed by these feelings. She was bent over, her nude body exposed to him, with the exception of the miniscule thong.

He placed a finger against his lips, warning her to maintain silence, his eyes glittering. He ran his hand down her back in a wonderful massage that left her feeling weak-kneed. Then his hand drifted down to her buttocks, which he also massaged. But when he pulled the crotch of her thong aside and a finger found the very center of her, she shot straight up and pressed her thighs together.

"I think we've gone far enough, Hunter. We're not accomplishing anything here." She hated the shaky sound of her voice as she shoved at his hand.

"Yes, we are. This is important. You need to learn to accept my touch, whenever, wherever. You need to *want* it." Hunter pressed down on her back again until she resumed the required position. "Stay put, now. Plant your palms on the mirror in front of you."

"I beg your pardon!" she hissed as she started straightening up again.

Again, he pressed down on her back, and landed an "I mean business" slap to her ass.

She opened her mouth to protest when he covered her mouth with a hand, keeping her bent over.

"Quiet," he murmured.

Glaring at him, she took a deep breath then nodded. He removed his hand and returned it to her ass, where he rubbed the still lingering sting away.

"I can't believe you just—you just—" She stuttered, couldn't say the word, but then added, "I wonder why you're revealing your perversions now, especially since I'd never seen so much as a clue of them during the two years we worked together. Is any of this necessary?"

"It is," his low voice rumbled. "Convincing those church folks of your devotion to me is important. And I can't think of a better way to show it than arousing you."

"Why don't you just ask me if that's possible?" she said.

"Because I know you. You'd say 'no' when you mean 'yes' because of your damned pride."

Regina felt him rub right up against her buttocks and she closed her eyes, stifling her groan of pleasure. Shivers slithered up her spine then down, pooling in the center of her body. A sting lingered in her ass from where he'd smacked her. Damn. But that sizzling feeling there made her want him to spank her again.

What was wrong with her!

Gently, he slid one finger inside her, then out, rimming her clit before repeating the delicious movement. Over and over his fingers worked their magic and she forgot about being embarrassed. Soon she closed her eyes at the exquisite sensations rippling through her body. *He wanted honest?* Well, she'd give it to him, and her hips began undulating in time with his touch. Heat filled her body, head to toe, when she felt wetness on the insides of her thighs.

He left her then, suddenly, and said brusquely, "You can straighten up now."

Regina rose, confused, unable to believe he'd stopped and left her wanting him—wanting more. Meeting his eyes in the mirror, she croaked out, "Well, what did you find out?"

"That you are attracted to me, whether you admit it or not. God, you're as wet and slippery as a seal's coat."

She sniffed. "Any man that did what you did would have the same results."

Hunter gave her a crooked, knowing little smile, followed by a smart slap to her ass again. "Yeah, right," he said dryly. Moving into position beside her, he faced the double-wide mirror, stared at her reflection, and said, "Take a look what you've done to me, Regina."

Her gaze slid down his body, pausing at his crotch. As she stared at the huge bulge in his jeans there was no doubt of his arousal.

Regina bit her lip as she maintained eye contact with his tormented expression that mirrored hers. "Hunter?" she said. "We could go back to my place, and mess—"

"I'll pay for the clothes while you're dressing," he muttered abruptly. He snatched up the clothing she'd modeled for him, then headed out of the dressing room.

She quickly dressed, hands shaking. While he completed the purchase, she fled the shop. Her humiliation was complete. With his dismissal, he'd reminded her that this was only a job, and that he wasn't the least bit interested in her personally. But then she thought about his own arousal, which he'd pointed out. Maybe she was wrong. She shook her head. No. Any man would have a bulge in his pants if he'd seen her dressed so scantily. Leaning back against the hood of his locked car she waited for him. Her eyes filled with tears as she stared down at the ground until a pair of men's brown loafers came into view. She couldn't meet his eyes at first and when she did, she couldn't conceal her disappointment.

She felt him staring at her as he opened the passenger door for her. She quickly settled into the seat. The drive home was accomplished in silence. Feeling decidedly uncomfortable, Regina had no idea how to proceed since Hunter hadn't said a word. Obviously, her feelings for him must be stronger than his were for her. She noticed his bulge had disappeared and now he didn't seem the least bit affected by the encounter.

When he pulled up in front of her house and turned to her, likely to tell her things just wouldn't work out—that she wasn't right for the job—she didn't stay to hear the words. She opened the door, hopped out of the car, and ran up the sidewalk.

CHAPTER FIVE

Hunter sighed as he watched her run up the sidewalk to her house. What could he say? She'd likely smack him upside the head if he approached her now. Hell, it was likely she'd never speak to him or have anything to do with him again. Could he blame her?

He should have eased her into the training he'd planned for her, training he knew she needed if they had any chance of convincing the people at the house that they were a couple madly in love with each other. He shouldn't have been so direct with her, but once he saw her clad in the corset in that damned dressing room, he'd changed his mind. He hadn't wanted to just feel her up, either; he'd wanted to fuck her, long and hard, taking her from the back with their eyes wide open and looking into that mirror. His cock hardened now at just the thought of it. Damn, he hoped he hadn't ruined things for she was perfect for this job.

She was perfect for him he mused, shaking his head. He shouldn't have smacked her ass, even though he had good reason since it was the perfect prelude to preparing her for the job. Even her indignant response to his swats raised his blood pressure, in a good way.

Then he thought about the clothing in his trunk and sighed. Hopefully he wouldn't have to return them.

That evening, as Hunter paced his hotel room, he tried to figure out what to do about Regina. He was baffled. He'd felt her arousal and knew she'd been caught up in the moment in the dressing room. He'd also seen the disappointment in her eyes, and the confusion when he hadn't given her the orgasm she'd expected. How could he explain why he hadn't? Regina was fairly innocent in the sex department he guessed and wouldn't know anything about orgasm denial to control a woman.

"Damn!" he growled, tunneling his fingers through his hair. He'd likely lost the best woman he'd ever find for the job. Several times in the past few hours he'd reached for the phone to call her but had stopped himself. If she still wanted to do the job she'd call, but he didn't expect her to. Already he started thinking of other possible candidates. Not a one he knew could measure up to Regina's talents and professionalism.

Later, he'd fallen asleep in the midst of a wild, erotic dream about Regina when his cell phone rang. He rolled over, snatched up the phone on the end table beside the bed and grumbled, "This had better be damned good."

"I need to do some reading for this assignment before we go any further."

Hunter's heart started pounding as he sat up at the sound of Regina's soft words. "I agree."

"Yeah, well, a promotion's important to me."

He frowned. Her promotion was the last thing on his mind. She wasn't giving an inch, nor had he expected her to. Deep down inside, he hoped she'd show or tell him how she felt about him—likely revulsion he decided, after what happened in the dressing room.

Now, after two years apart, he realized he felt differently about Regina. Not being married any longer was likely the reason, he decided.

When they finished this job, he'd show her his sensitive side. *Yeah, right, buddy, like you've ever had one?* According to his ex-wife he never had.

"I've a trunk full of books for you to check out. I'll drop them by tomorrow. But let me email you some of those websites also for you to look over. Lots of information on those, too."

"Okay. I'll watch for the list. Don't come until five or so. The station's short-handed."

He sighed. "Your chief said you were all mine for the rest of the week and until after the job's done."

"They need me tomorrow."

He grumbled, "Damn, well, only tomorrow. Hmm, that's right around supper time—five..."

"Don't push your luck," she said.

Hunter chuckled. "I wasn't suggesting you feed me again. How about I take you out to dinner? We can discuss some of the books that I think you should read that will help?"

"Sure. I'll meet you at the Grand Avenue Grill on Grand and Tenth around five-fifteen."

CHAPTER SIX

The next afternoon, Regina arrived at the grill fifteen minutes late. As luck would have it, just minutes before going off her second shift of the day, she'd answered a call to the shopping strip on Sixth and Elm.

A high school student, one of several who'd recently completed the 'Dare Program' (Drug Abuse Resistant Education), had been caught smoking marijuana standing outside a store, nonchalant as can be, as though it were nothing more than a cigarette. Blatantly disregarding the law, the boy, the only son of one of the wealthiest men in the city, pretty much told her to go screw herself. She'd replied by shoving him into the back of her police car and driving him over to the station where she then called his mom and dad. The parents arrived, none too happy with their son or with her, for that matter. Like it was her fault the kid was a spoiled brat and had a habit?

The grill was quiet but then it was early and 'happy hour' hadn't started yet.

"Hi," she said as she sank into a booth at the very back of the restaurant, opposite Hunter who was sipping a beer. She grabbed the menu, gave it a cursory perusal then tossed it on the end of the table. It took her a moment to realize he hadn't said a word.

She glanced up, met his stone-faced expression. Lifting one eyebrow, she said, "What?"

"You're late."

"Couldn't be helped. Something came up at the last minute, and—"

"Don't let it happen again," he growled.

Her brow went up. "Well, *excuse* me." She sank back in her seat and when she crossed one leg over the other, she kicked him. "Sorry," she murmured.

Regina kept her expression passive, somewhat brooding, even though a smile threatened to split her face at the narrow-eyed look he gave her. Had he known she'd kicked him intentionally?

He wore black well, she decided, taking in his short-sleeved black t-shirt that showed off his well-developed chest. Though she couldn't see him below the waist, she guessed he wore black jeans as well. His dark hair was combed in its rakish, usual way. The guy had his own style all right, and it was timeless. Most women would be salivating right now, but not her. Uh-uh. *Right.*

Bristling as she thought about his curt comment, she said, "Are you going to talk to me or what?"

"Are you going to be late again?"

She noted his fine-chiseled lips pressed together, eyes hard and unyielding. *What gives,* she wondered? He was demanding, arrogant and cold. Then it came to her; he was playing a part!

Okay, it was her turn. She ducked her head and murmured, "Sorry. It won't happen again."

Her head shot up when she heard what sounded suspiciously like choking. She watched a slow grin cross his lips and smiled, too, even as he swiped a froth of beer from his mouth with the palm of his hand.

Giving him an innocent, wide-eyed look, she said, "Well, isn't that what you wanted? Me, subservient and apologetic?"

With a cocky smirk, he said, "Actually, I was sort of hoping you wouldn't catch on so fast."

"Now why would you want that? We do want to rescue Miss Matthews, don't we?"

"Of course. I just thought I'd have some fun along the way."

"At my expense?"

He shrugged. "Don't think you'll avoid being punished because of a mere apology."

"Oh, come off it, Hunter, enough play-acting."

"I'm not pretending," he said softly, leveling his eyes on her.

"Don't tell me my ex-partner's a closet Dominant," she scoffed.

He just stared at her.

"No way!" she blared.

He shrugged again. "Believe what you will, though you'll find out the truth of it soon enough. Don't you wonder why I know so much about this house, and its inhabitants' lifestyles?"

"Thought you said you interviewed some past clients."

"I did. They also happened to be close friends of mine."

Regina ignored her misgivings. "So, if it's true, is this why Sheila divorced you?"

"No," he said flatly.

Regina couldn't figure him out even though she'd known him for a while. No way would he know about kinky stuff like this, except, possibly, in the line of duty. And they'd never paid a call to any BDSM establishments while working together. Since he insisted they stay in their roles, she would play along.

Then she thought about Sheila. "So, why did you get divorced?"

He sank against the back of the booth. "Not open for discussion. That's your second infraction meaning you've earned another punishment on top of the first."

Regina sighed. "I'd really like to know what happened."

His voice was stern. "Off limits, Regina."

She couldn't help being curious, still she was relieved when the waitress arrived. She opened her mouth, ready to order when Hunter ordered burgers, salads, and beer, for both of them.

Her eyes opened wide as she stared at him.

He met her eyes. "What?"

"I could have ordered myself," she bristled.

"Get used to it."

"You ordering for me?"

"Among other things, yes. Would you have ordered something different?"

"No."

"Well, there you have it." Leaning forward, he added, "I know you well enough to know you would have ordered the same thing."

She rolled her eyes. "True, still, I feel like I'm suddenly living in the 50's, for god's sake," she grumbled. Looking at him she noticed his smile widen yet he remained quiet.

The silence unnerved her, though, and after a while she asked, "You mad at me?"

"No, just waiting for you to open up the conversation again. You know, your curiosity has always been the bane of your existence, and mine, I might add."

She grinned. "True, but it's helped me and you in and out of tight situations in the past."

"I'll tell you about Sheila, sometime, but not now. I want us to concentrate on this job."

"I'm all for that," she said. "The sooner we enter that place and rescue your client, the sooner we'll be done."

The food arrived, and they ate with little conversation between them. When they finished Regina wasn't surprised Hunter had come prepared. He reached into a duffel bag on the seat beside him and pulled out a book, then two more. The first title he held up for her inspection, bound side facing her was called, *The Submissive Life* by Arianna.

She glanced around self-consciously, glad to see they were the only ones seated at the back of the grill. Still she grabbed the book from his hand and smacked it down on the table. "Advertise, why don't you?"

He just smiled.

She started flipping through the pages. After a few moments, she shoved the book toward Hunter. She gulped and thought about the woman's submissive words in relationship to her dominant husband in the book, and the explicit, sexual photographs, including several with the pretty, middle-aged Arianna settled face-down over her husband's lap, his hand raised high over her naked buttocks. "I'm not so sure I can do this."

"Give it your best shot. You're a pro. And everyone's got a darker side—just let it take over."

"Darker side?"

He nodded, his eyes delving deep into hers. Then he took her hand and pulled. Soon she found herself sitting beside him in the booth. She struggled half-heartedly to put some distance between them, emitting a surprised shriek when he slid his hand down between her thighs.

"Yes," he murmured, his words soft and suggestive. "Imagine something infinitely deeper, darker than just making traditional love; something unimaginably tempting and hedonistic."

His fingers began to slide up the inside of her thigh. Then, upon reaching its destination, did a tap dance across her clit. Even through the soft, worn cloth of her uniform pants, it immediately swelled and started to throb. Within moments she slumped against the back of the booth, exquisitely defeated as she gave into his magical touch.

Closing her eyes, caught up in the moment of heady desire, she sat on the edge, awaiting the rush of heat and anticipation of what she expected to feel—a wrenching orgasm. Suddenly his fingers stopped moving and left her. She opened her eyes, stunned, anger building as she watched him pick up his mug, tip his head back and swallow down his beer.

She scrambled from the booth and glared down at him, her breasts heaving in fury. "Why did you do that?" she gasped. "Why did you stop?"

Hunter slammed his mug down on the table. "Sit down and stop making a scene," he murmured, his eyes riveted on her.

Her hands fisted at her sides as she covertly looked around, saw people watching them. Turning to him again, she said, "I'll be damned if I sit and listen to you anymore. I want an answer."

A grin flitted across his lips as he folded his arms and sank against the back of the booth. "I must be making an impression on you. You're swearing."

"Tell me," she hissed.

"Haven't figured it out yet? Surprising, since you've always been a quick study."

Regina leaned down and stabbed a finger in the center of his chest. "You know I'm quick—quicker than you, for sure."

Regina thought about how quickly she'd reacted when he'd been shot; how she'd moved impossibly fast to apprehend the perp. At the time, she knew she'd be damned if she allowed the best partner she'd ever had die on her. He'd lived but she had stayed with him until paramedics arrived, allowing the perp to get free. But it was the right call at the time.

"You're right. I admit it," he said. "Sit down and I'll fill you in on where I'm heading."

Giving him the most grudging look she could muster she sank into the seat across from him again and clasped her hands in front of her on the table.

Leaning forward, he reached out and took her hands in both of his, pulling her toward him.

Stunned by the gentle move, she savored the feeling of his big hands holding hers and listened to his explanation.

"In the house, that's one of the ways they train men to keep their women in line."

She gulped. "I…I don't understand."

"The idea is that if you sexually deprive a woman, she'll be completely obedient and follow all orders in order to be given the ultimate gift—orgasm."

Her face turned hot. "You've got to be kidding," she gasped.

Hunter shook his head. "Nope." His laughter filled the restaurant.

"Stop it," she muttered and yanked her hands away from him "Are you sure about this?"

Hunter settled that intimate, dark-eyed look on her once more. "I interviewed enough couples who had stayed at the house in the past and been told this by each couple."

"So, this is all part of the 'act.' Right?"

His only reply was, "Want another beer?"

"No."

"One's enough for me, too."

Regina flipped through the book and read several interesting passages, conscious of Hunter's eyes on her. Finally, she snapped the book shut. All she wanted to do was get home, get into bed, and read the book cover to cover. Though she'd never admit it to anyone but herself, the little she'd read was—titillating. She sighed at her perverse thoughts and decided she'd been without a man for too long.

"I'll take this home and study it," she murmured, checking the time on her watch. "I need to get going."

He was quiet—too quiet, and she nearly jumped out of her seat when he did speak after a long moment's silence.

"Look at me, Regina."

She met his eyes and lifted her chin.

"How'd the date go the other night?"

"Date?"

"You told me—"

"Uh…oh, the date!" She waved her hand negligently. "No big deal, really."

"You didn't answer my question," he persisted.

"Listen, if we want to find Matilda, I've got to crack the books." She picked up the stack and scrambled from the booth.

"Be honest. When was the last time you were involved with someone?"

Regina glared down at him. "You're not going to drop this, are you?"

"Nope."

"Two years," she said.

"Ah," he said, satisfied. "That explains things. So there was no date."

She shook her head. "Explains what?"

"How you nearly exploded beneath my fingers a few moments ago, within a surprisingly short amount of time and little effort on my part, not to mention what happened back in that dressing room, and—"

She sputtered, "Now wait just a damned minute—"

"Bad language twice in the same day? I'm shocked. You'll be punished for that, also, and for lying to me about the date."

She rubbed her temples. "I'm confused," she murmured then raised her gaze to his now filled with humor. "*You're* confusing me."

"How so?"

"I never know if you're serious or if you're acting."

"Just always believe that whatever I say I mean it."

He came to his feet and left money on the table. Then he took her hand and escorted her outside. Though it was early evening, the air was still as hot and muggy as it had been during the day. Regina didn't look forward to another restless night of sleep since her air-conditioning had broken down, and she hadn't had a chance to call someone to fix it.

Stopping beside her car he wound his arms around her then plastered a mind-boggling kiss on her lips. Regina melted in his arms as she enjoyed the heady sensations.

When he released her, he stepped back and stared at her. He seemed to be gauging her reaction, she decided. He'd affected her, no doubt about it, yet she kept her feelings tucked deep inside her, kept a passive expression on her face.

He gave her a wry look. "I'll be by your house tomorrow to see what you've learned, and to finish off where we left off tonight, including introducing you to the punishments you've earned. I'll call you first. Oh, also, we need to go over the contract from The House."

"Contract?" she asked, confused.

"Yes, we have to both read the rules and regs and sign that we agree with them."

"Isn't it simply sign and write a check over to them?"

"We have to read it thoroughly," he groused. "Tomorrow."

She opened her mouth to reply when he strode away. My, Lord, he'd left as though nothing had happened; left her in a puddle of longing and confusion. Finally gathering her wits, she shouted after him, "Come after supper. I'm not cooking for you again."

He whirled around and, walking backwards and said, "Yes, you will. Until we've finished this job, you'll be *my* woman and that includes taking care of *my* needs." He turned and loped the few steps to his car, leaving her speechless.

Oh, how she wished she had a baseball to throw at his head! What a stubborn, arrogant brute, she mused. Then she sighed. Damn, it was that acting again. She had to learn to stay in the 'part' and learn to accept the fact none of this was true, but only fiction.

Hitting the button on her car's remote to unlock the door, she sank behind the wheel and sighed. It was true that the man irked her, but he also excited her. She couldn't recall when she'd felt such a strong attraction toward a man. She asked herself what made him different than other guys but couldn't come up with an answer.

She had to admit it was chemistry—plain and simple. She'd felt it when they had been partners, and it had returned full force now that they were working together again. Or the guy had missed his calling and should have been an actor. He was very convincing playing his part.

CHAPTER SEVEN

The following afternoon, Regina groaned as she sank behind the wheel of her PT Cruiser. It had been another scorching day, and a record day for ticketing folks, in particular, teen-agers. Thank God school would begin in a month. Most of the tickets she'd issued had been for speeding. Her beat had started at 6:00 a.m. and ended now, at 2:30 p.m. She felt grimy and sweaty from head to toe. A long, cool shower was what she needed. Just the thought of it gave her the impetus to turn the key and drive home.

With so many of her fellow workers either on vacation or out sick, she'd been called in again for day duty when she was supposed to be working with Hunter. She shrugged. At least she had the remainder of the day and evening to work with him.

She checked in at the station and clocked out just as Chief Sanchez was leaving.

"Off to a meeting, chief?" Regina asked, knowing full well her boss never left before five p.m.

The chief sank against the doorjamb and Regina caught the exhaustion on her face. "Yes, with the mayor this time. Again." Looking at Regina closely, she asked, "Why are you here and not on the job with Monroe?" She smiled then and added, "Changed your mind?"

"The captain called me in saying the force was short-handed

today. Besides, I haven't officially accepted the job yet." She blew out a breath. "This is going to be a tough one, so I'm on the fence yet." Heat flushed through Regina's face as she looked at the sly look in the chief's eyes.

"I heard. Before you came in, Monroe told me all about it." Her gaze swept over Regina. "You can do it. I know you can. Think about the benefits of the job."

Had Hunter informed the chief of their arrangement? "Benefits?"

"I don't mean the money and promotion," she said, chuckling. Then she turned on her stiletto heel and swung out the door, throwing over her shoulder, "Good luck, Officer Arrigoni."

Regina scowled, confused. What was that chuckle about? She groaned; it was obvious Monroe had told the chief the fine details of the job. She strode out the door and made her way to her car, fury tearing through her that he'd divulge this information to her superior.

Ten minutes later she turned into her driveway, saw Hunter's car, and groaned. *Not now.* She'd texted him not to come over until 7:00 p.m. Did the man ever listen to her? She stormed inside and found him in the kitchen.

"What are you doing here? And how did you get into my house? You better not have broken one of my windows."

He was in the process of unloading her dishwasher which to her mind would make any woman happy. She wasn't. He'd managed to get inside her locked house and that didn't sit well with her.

Straightening up he glanced at her before turning to a cupboard where he'd already put away several glasses. "I grabbed a house key off your key holder before I left after supper the other evening." Raising his brow, he added, "You shouldn't leave them out in plain sight."

Damn, she mused, disgusted with herself; both because of her new penchant for swearing and because he was right. She loved country-style decorating objects and had found an adorable cow-shaped wooden key holder that hung from a chain on the end of her cupboard. It would have been easy for him to reach out and grab a key from the hook. But it was theft, pure and simple. She should arrest him. She smiled at the thought of clamping a pair of handcuffs on him. Oh, what she would love to do to the man when restrained.

Extending a glass of wine to her, he said, "Here. You look as though you need it."

"Thanks." Taking the glass, she swallowed a healthy sip then loosened her tie as she headed out of the kitchen and down the hallway. "I'm hot and in need of a shower. I want you gone by the time I'm done."

A chuckle drifted after her, and he said, "We've work to do first."

Regina hadn't been truthful with her boss. She'd had plenty of time over the past twenty-four hours to think about the promotion and concluded it wasn't all that important to her. After having read through the books, she decided she'd fail miserably playing the role of submissive. Hunter would need to find another woman for the part, but not until she tried once more. One final time.

As she undressed, she thought about the submissive Arianna and shivered at the thought of behaving like her. It would be impossible, yet something simmered deep inside her; the thought that she *could* do it, and that she'd enjoy the role of submissive. The problem was the other player; she wasn't sure she could accept Hunter's domination. Perhaps if he loved her as she had loved him when she left Chicago—as she loved him now—it would be easier. She was certain she still carried that torch for him but add in lust now and it was even worse.

Yet, she asked herself how could she allow him to do those things Arianna allowed her husband to do? It would be impossible to separate acting from reality, but she'd try, once more.

Shrugging into a white terry cloth robe she took several more sips of wine, wondering what vintage it was, enjoying the sweet-bitter taste of it. Usually she liked her wine dryer, but the sweet flavor of this one was enjoyable. She finished the glass and called out, "Hey, Hunter! Pour me another while I shower and bring it in here!"

She felt relaxed and cozy from the hot water flowing over her body. Donning her robe again she exited the bathroom and found another glass of the red wine on her dresser and took a few more healthy swallows.

She sat on the edge of her bed and closed her eyes, lethargy overwhelming her. Hot showers always left her feeling drowsy, but after this one she couldn't keep her eyes open. She decided just a moment's rest was all she needed to revive her since it was much too early for bed. Lying on her bed she fell instantly asleep and didn't feel the glass slipping from her hand to the carpeting.

She wakened slowly, drowsiness still clouding her head, groaning as wondrous tickling sensations hardened her nipples, spreading in larger and larger concentric circles around her breasts. Soft, gentle flicks one moment then harder ones, sent shivers through her body and her vulva began to throb. She was having difficulty opening her eyes, too. What was wrong with her?

Eventually, she managed to pry them open and squinted at Hunter, who leaned over her body. She followed his hand as it traveled across every inch of her skin, leaving a trail of heat and desire in its wake. She felt unbelievably horny—more so than the other times he'd touched her.

Her tiredness prompted her to think she'd been drugged. Regina recognized that feeling for she'd unknowingly been drugged once before in her law enforcement career while performing undercover work on the force with Hunter.

The thought that he'd drugged her made her frown; made her think she needed to pull herself out of her stupor, but she couldn't. Whatever he had dropped into that wine had been powerful, offering aphrodisiac qualities for the shivers and tingles tearing through her body made her lose her inhibitions.

Her words were slurred when she said, "What did you slip into my wine?"

His brow shot up as he sat back. "Nothing."

"Oh, come on," she groaned. "I've been drugged before. I'm horny as hell, and don't tell me it's just from the wine."

"It must be. The only drugs I know that act like an aphrodisiac are illegal. I didn't spike your wine. It's a new vintage I picked up at Haroldson's on the way over here." He frowned. "Maybe you're just sensitive to it. Tell me what you're feeling," he encouraged her.

She narrowed her eyes on him thoughtfully. "Like I said, I'm horny. My nipples are tender, for one thing."

He grinned. "You saw me when you woke up. I was stroking them."

"Darn it, Hunter!" Regina shook her head and the world started spinning. She covered her mouth with her hand and her words were muffled. "God, I hope I'm not going to be sick!"

With a frown, he said, "Me too," and scooped her up in his arms and headed for the bathroom. They made it just in time for Regina to lose her late lunch and the wine. Hanging over the toilet bowl she gave him a sideways look through squinty eyes. "You sure you didn't put anything in it?"

"You know I'd never do anything like that to you," he snapped. "I had a beer and feel fine. Must have been the wine. Got to be something wrong with it so I'm pouring out the rest."

She watched him stride out of the bathroom and even though she was feeling utterly sick and useless she admired him in his blue jeans. She hung over the toilet bowl once more before leaving the bathroom and crawling beneath the covers on her bed where oblivion found her.

———

What the hell? Regina raised her head and looked at the clock on the bedside table. "3:00 a.m.," she whispered, then groaned aloud. She plopped her head back down on her pillow, reached up and rubbed her temples. Better, she felt better, she decided, except for the nagging headache.

She threw out her arm and hit something. Carefully, she turned to her other side and found Hunter beside her, arms thrown over his head as he lay on a pillow. Her eyes moved down slowly, taking in his naked, toned chest. Lifting herself onto an elbow, her hand tucked against her head, she perused him once more, until she met his eyes.

The bedside light suddenly went on and she found him grinning at her. "Enjoying the view?"

Heat settled inside her at the sensual look on his face, and she squeaked when he put his hands around her waist and hauled her on top of him, smacking her ass.

"Hunter," she protested, "I...I have a headache." She felt the heat of him, not to mention a pole between them jabbing against her stomach.

"Try something more original."

"Would you stop doing that?" she whined.

"Doing what?"

"You know what! Stop hitting my ass. It hurts," she grumbled.

"If you're sore from those couple love taps at the clothing store you are a lightweight." Grinning devilishly, he added, "I'll have to toughen you up."

She ignored his comment. "Stop being such a beast. And why are you in my bed?"

"Seemed as good a place as any to sleep, seeing as we're together now."

"But—"

He wagged his finger in her face. "We *are* together, until this job is done. Besides, I gave up my hotel reservation to stay with you."

When she didn't reply but simply rolled her eyes at him, his hand landed with a loud slap against her ass once more. She gasped, jammed her hands against his shoulders and pushed. He wouldn't release her. The stinging in her ass reminded her that she was bare butt naked. *Her ass was bare! Her plump ass.*

"Did you...undress me?"

"Sure did, and with great pleasure." His grin slid away, and Regina saw a passion light up his eyes. "If you were truly mine, I wouldn't allow you to wear any clothes while we're home together."

She sniffed. "Well, I'm not yours, so sorry to disappoint you."

"You are, until the job's done, or did you forget about the job? So, don't bother getting dressed because we're going to start practicing tomorrow."

Changing the subject quickly, she said, "I need to get more sleep since I have to work in the morning."

"I had a talk with your captain last night, and he decided he won't need you until after you've completed this assignment with me. Everyone's back from vacation now, he said."

"You had no right to do that," she growled.

Frowning, he rolled her off him. Scrambling up into a sitting position, she snatched the sheet up to her breasts and saw he wore his boxer-briefs. Noted the pole once more when her eyes landed on his prominent bulge. He rose from the bed and stood before her, legs spread, arms crossed over his chest.

"I am on a timeframe to complete this job, and you've been working the last few days at your normal job and not with me. Now we have an agreement between us, right?"

He glared down at her with his hands on his hips. Leaning sideways, she grumped, "Okay, got it, yes, we have an agreement."

"All right. The House emailed me the contract for us to sign. I'd like you to read it—thoroughly—it's quite lengthy."

"Don't need to read it. Just tell me where to sign."

"Never sign anything without reading it first."

She waved her hand in the air and sank back on her pillow. "No need. I trust you. Besides, most contracts are all the same—yada, yada."

He sighed. "All right, don't blame me if there's something in it you don't like, after the fact."

He left the bedroom and returned a few minutes later. He turned the pages—the many pages—and Regina watched him, her eyes widening "What in the hell? They write a damned book of instructions?"

He chuckled. "Yeah, sort of."

"Here's the signing page."

She sat up again, eyes barely open, grabbed the pen from him and signed on a line right below his signature.

"I can't sleep so I'm getting up to do some work."

She groaned, watched him with contract in hand. "It's the middle of the night, and I don't wanna get up," she protested.

He finished slipping on his jeans over his fine, lean hips. "You get more rest since you were pretty sick last night. That's one thing I have to do today—have that bottle of wine checked out."

"I thought you said you were throwing it down the drain?"

"Nope, kept it to have it tested."

"Excellent idea. Later," she murmured as she rolled onto her stomach and jammed her arms around her pillow, heaving a deep sigh.

———

Five hours later, Regina woke up to the sun shining through the blinds. Hadn't she shut those last night? Then she groaned when she saw Hunter sitting on the end of the bed with a cup of coffee in his hand.

She sat up and frowned at him. "Did you just wake me up by opening the blinds?" she groused.

"Yup, time to get some practice in for the day." He handed over the coffee. "We need to brush up on your acting skills. Training time begins in fifteen minutes."

Regina inhaled the coffee aroma then raised her eyes to meet his. "You always did know how to make a good cup of coffee."

He just smiled, sat there, and watched her drink.

"I managed to get a hold of the liquor store. Unfortunately, you weren't the only one who got sick, so I filed a report with them. They'd already run tests on that wine and found it bacteria-ridden. Funny it tasted fine." He shrugged. "As long as you're okay nothing more we can do now."

"Even my headache went away," she said.

He stood up and she slid her gaze over his jeans-clad legs. He also wore a short-sleeved gray polo shirt that showcased the smooth muscles in his arms. Damn, he looked good—even his bare feet.

"If you could have a second cup ready when I come out, I'd appreciate it. I'll get dressed first."

She sat there the sheet raised up to her breasts as she waited for him to leave.

Looking around her room, he nodded. "You know, I don't know what I was expecting your bedroom to look like since you'd painted the outside of your house purple, but I like what you've done in here."

She'd used neutral, creamy, and sunny yellow colors in her bedroom, from the walls, to the blinds on the windows, white trim around the windows and baseboard, and a white comforter. It was soothing, and he appreciated the art deco type photos on the wall.

"Thanks," she said.

"Don't bother getting dressed." He turned and headed for the door.

Her voice squeaked, "Excuse me?"

He paused, hand on the doorknob. "I know you don't have a hearing problem. I said, no clothes."

"You can't be—"

"Serious?" At her slow nod, he added, "Damned serious. This is an important part of the training. If I say you wear no clothes, you don't. If I say you deserve punishment, you do. If I say eat, you will. If I say take a nap, you'll do it. If I say don't get yourself off—that's for me to decide—you won't. Get it?"

Regina saw he was dead serious, and she gave him a slow nod. She felt a stream of heat flushing through her body at the thought of being naked while he 'trained her.'

He narrowed his eyes on her. "On second thought, dig out and dress in that little black number you picked up on our shopping trip."

As she watched him, she remembered it, of course, she'd had to have it. The black corset, thong and long black stockings held up by the garters attached to the black corset, and the high heels. Oh yeah, she'd have to wear the heels as then she'd be as tall as him.

As she sat in bed contemplating wearing the sexy outfit as

they worked, she closed her eyes and gulped. But then she thought this was Hunter she was working with, not a stranger. Also, she knew he'd take a bullet for her. She could trust him. She could do this job.

Jumping from the bed she brushed her teeth, her hair, then pulled the pieces out of her closet where she'd hung them. She dressed quickly and slipped on the heels. A quick glance in the mirror on her closet door let her know she looked every bit as sexy as she had wearing the outfit in the shop. Then, turning around, she cringed at the view of her body in the thong, the corset stopped at her waistline, exposing the twin cheeks of her ass, just the narrow fabric of the thong between her butt cheeks showing.

Throwing her shoulders back, she grabbed up her robe, in case she lost her nerve, and sauntered out of her bedroom, saw her next steaming cup of coffee on the island and headed for it. Right when she reached for it, he intercepted her. He leaned against the island, one leg crossed over the other, coffee in hand. She frowned and noted he'd removed his shirt.

"What?" she asked as her eyes widened on the tattoo that wrapped around one bicep, then slithered down the left side of his chest to his stomach. It was a dragon, its tail around his bicep, its body curling down over his broad chest and then its head ending below his navel.

She'd seen him bare-chested before and decided it was new for she would have seen it before now. She shivered at the thought of all of those fine needles pricking her skin. She was far from being a pain-slut. There was no way she'd ever pay to get a tattoo.

He made a little circle in front of him. "Turn around."

"You saw when I came out," she snapped as she draped the robe across the island.

He set the cup down with a sigh and she snatched it up.

"You need to get comfortable being naked or in other states of undress around me." He crossed his arms across his broad chest. "We're married, remember?"

Rolling her eyes, she stepped back, cup in hand, then crossed one foot over the other and pivoted. She faced away from him, started to pivot again when his big hands landed on her hips. She closed her eyes, felt him brush up against her back.

"Very nice," he drawled.

She gasped when his hand brushed down her back, and over her ass, to which he gave a little pat. Scrunching her eyes tight she stayed quiet as he spoke, his lips whispering against her ear.

"Like I said, you need to be comfortable with me in order to convince folks you're my surrendered wife."

Looking over her shoulder at him, she asked, "Excuse me?"

"You heard me—surrendered—submissive."

She widened her eyes as she watched him saunter over to her divan and sink down. Then she gasped when she saw a ping-pong sized leather paddle beside him, on the end table.

Where in the hell had that come from?

He picked up the thin, flexible black leather and smacked it against one palm where it made a distinct, loud slapping sound.

Her eyes lingered on the paddle, and suddenly chills swept over her body, and she felt a slick, wet heat between her thighs. Her voice trembled as she met the intent look in his eyes. "You can't mean to use that on me."

"Yep. Punishment first, then we'll work on other stuff."

Her eyes widened as she tried to think of an excuse. "What about breakfast?"

"You didn't have shit in your refrigerator, so I stopped by the store while you were sleeping. I'll make you a big breakfast in about an hour. Now, sweet pea. Over my knee."

She smacked her cup down on the island so hard the remaining coffee splashed over the side. "No."

"Come here. Now," he said in that soft, deep voice she'd only heard a few times of late. "One of the first things we'll do upon entering The House of Christian Love is show them that you wish me to be head of our household, and you will submit to punishment when they believe it's warranted. They have a welcome evening for members, a public display of husbands of new members disciplining their wives. Together. In the same room."

She gasped, "No way."

"Yes, way. You signed that contract. Remember?"

She squirmed. She had, damn it. "And is that specifically in the contract? This initiation or whatever the hell you call it?"

"Yep, it sure is. Told you to read before you signed."

"And I'm supposed to take it like the meek little wifie that I am, quietly, no protests?"

He shook his head and slid his arms along the back of the sofa, the paddle still in his right hand. "Hell, no. You can scream, protest, cry, show your emotions. No one would expect you to be silent."

"Why is that?"

"Because it will be—painful—though I'll try and back off somewhat, but this has to look real so we're *really* going to do this."

She twisted her hands, bit her lip as she tried to find an excuse but couldn't.

Hunter sighed. "Think about that promotion and no credit card debt. Think of what a great feeling that will be. You're not a quitter, Regina, never have been. Come on. It won't be so bad." He set the paddle down beside him on the sofa.

"For you it won't be!" she exploded. She eyed him sitting there with his eyebrows raised, his hot eyes on her, a glimmer of a smile on his face. Damn, was he getting off on this?

Stop thinking about it and just do it. The reward's worth it. If anyone would have to grin and bear it, it would be him since she noticed how he couldn't seem to stop sliding his gaze up and down her body with keen appreciation.

Throwing her shoulders back she stalked over to him, bent over and settled herself over his knees. She planted her hands on the floor, her hair swiping it as she took a deep breath. *What in the hell was she doing?*

CHAPTER EIGHT

"Beautiful," he murmured, his eyes sweeping over her corset once more before adjusting her over his thighs.

Heat flared through him at the sight of Regina's voluptuous body. She was tall and gorgeous, and his for a short while.

Her ass was a piece of work—sublime, he mused, as he lightly caressed her bottom cheeks. At his first touch he heard her gasp, felt her stiffen under his hand, still he kept his hand on her ass, squeezing it, enjoying her way too much more than he should, but he couldn't help himself. He felt his arousal, knew his cock was hard already, even before laying on the first smack. Even when he'd hit the BDSM clubs when he had free time, wherever his work took him, he'd never seen any other woman's ass compare to hers. Creamy smooth, solid yet plump.

The thong with its narrow piece of black fabric separating her full globes mesmerized him, as did the creamy skin, which he knew he'd be reddening. Her ass was meant to be punished, meant to fall under his hand, a crop, paddle, hairbrush...and the list went on forever as he thought about different implements he could use to enhance the color of her cheeks.

She wiggled on his lap and he picked up the paddle, landing a sharp slap on one cheek. "Hold still."

She gasped but obeyed. He shifted her body forward, until her ass was higher over his knee, her torso dangling, her hair brushing the carpet. Positioned perfectly for her punishment, with her ass in the air, it was way past time they started practicing. In two days, he'd scheduled their interview so there was little time to prepare.

"Now, then," he said casually, as he settled the paddle on her ass again and made light circles, "how many do you think you deserve?"

She was silent for a bit and he knew she was thinking. He also knew she'd provide a low number, which he of course would raise.

"None," she said drolly.

Again, he landed a sharp smack. She gasped again, and he said, "Wrong answer. Try again."

"Five?" she whispered, tightening her hold on his calf.

Leaning to one side, he looked at her long, wavy hair hanging down, covering her face like a veil around her. Remembering he'd placed a hair binder in his pocket, he dug for it, then swept up her hair and fashioned it into a low ponytail at the nape of her neck.

"From now on, as we work on our roles, tie your hair up or back."

She didn't reply but he saw her nod.

Holding a submissive's ponytail when he dished out discipline, or had sex, was satisfying. He hadn't been in a club in almost a year and he was thrilled to be back in the saddle again, yet never had he imagined it being with Regina.

As he looked down at her slightly pinkened skin he came to a decision and set the paddle down beside him once more. Fisting her ponytail, he pulled her head up a bit. "Ten with my hand first. And with the paddle, we'll decide as we go."

"What the hell, Hunter!" she groaned.

"Unless we add more for profanity," he growled. Stroking her ass, he added, "From now on call me Sir."

She chuckled wryly, then said, "I will not—"

His palm crashed down hard enough it jolted her forward

while his other hand yanked back on her ponytail. Her scream told him she'd definitely felt it.

"When we're at The House of Christian Love, that's a requirement. Start using it now, every time you start to say my name replace it with Sir."

He frowned when he saw, already, a faint reddening in her cheeks, and just from a few slaps. Virgin butts always showed color after just a few swats, he knew, but by the time they left The House of Christian Love, she wouldn't have a virgin ass any longer.

"Now we begin."

"Wait a minute!" she shouted. "Those count, right?"

"Nope, darlin', we start from scratch." He raised his hand and lightly smacked her right cheek, delighting in watching how her curvy globes jiggled. She had quieted, which meant she likely could take it harder. He stepped up the intensity, testing her pain level, raising his arm higher and coming down with a sharp staccato tempo. Soon her legs were kicking, and she pinched his calf. He'd reached seven.

"Stop digging your nails into my leg," he ordered, pausing.

"It hurts!" she protested as she covered her ass with one hand.

"Hmm, I'd thought you'd have a higher pain tolerance, or maybe you're just faking it?" He grasped her wrist and settled it at the small of her back, then spanked her sit spot three more times as he counted, "Eight, nine, ten."

He released her hand, surprised she hadn't made more fuss, and he sank back, giving her a break, smoothing his hand over pinkened skin. He noted her shoulders relaxed then, releasing her tensed up muscles, and when she started to rise, he held her down with a hand on her lower back.

"That was ten, but that was just my hand. I decided on ten with the paddle," he said as he picked it up from the sofa.

She groaned when he asked softly, "Ready?"

Going limp as a dishrag, she nodded.

Not giving her a chance to think much more, he quickly laid the first five on her with the paddle, the whippy slaps resounding in the room. He felt his cock harden beneath her, closed his eyes a moment in order to keep control, though the feeling was unbelievably erotic—felt damned good. Fuck, that's what he wanted to do—was fuck her—which ultimately happened whenever he was involved in a discipline scene with a sub at a club.

She had managed to remain quiet this time, but that wouldn't do.

"As I mentioned, the folks at the house would expect to hear you crying, so let loose."

She glanced at him over her shoulder, a scowl on her face. "Aren't we done?"

With that sassy attitude, she needed more.

"I want to see some tears," he ordered. "I'll keep doing this until I see them, got it?"

She snapped, "You didn't mention that as a criteria to end this. You said ten with the paddle!"

He smacked her ass once with the paddle. She cringed. "It is. I should have mentioned it."

"So, you're saying if I need to fake it I should, right?"

"Right. I've no idea of what your pain tolerance is, and everyone is different. Just pretend like you're going for an academy award."

Closing her eyes tightly, she nodded once more and looked down at the floor.

Hunter knew the whippy black leather paddle stung like the dickens, worse than his hand, but he couldn't back down now. Lucky for her he'd used just his hand for the first part of the count. She needed to learn to listen and obey him, for their safety. He also had to see her distress—her tears—to be believable. Knowing this, he knew he had to make these next ones count.

Winding his legs around hers, he captured them, so she couldn't free herself—or kick him. He hoped that once he administered this final punishment, she'd cry real tears and obey him instantly, so he wouldn't have to punish her this harshly when next time he gave her an order. Also, she'd earned this punishment as she'd lied to him, something a sub shouldn't do. This punishment, hopefully, would cure her of that.

"No more lying," he said. Holding her wrist behind her back, he raised his arm high and whipped off the final five, the snap of the paddle precisely on her sit spot where her bottom cheeks and thighs met, alternating cheeks again, the sharp sound of the slaps exploding in the room.

He heard her breath catch as she wriggled against him, trying to escape from the first moment of the second slap. Her shoulders shook, and she sniffled, still clutched one hand onto his jeans-clad calf.

"Stop, Hunt—Sir," she gritted out.

Frowning, he leaned forward and saw a stream of tears dripping down each cheek. He heaved a sigh of relief, glad for her tears—satisfaction tearing through him at her distress. He guessed these weren't fake tears, but the real thing.

He should be satisfied she'd followed orders this time as she'd need to on the job, still, he questioned himself—had he been too hard on her? Looking down at the once pale skin of her virginal, perfect ass, he saw he'd reddened it but there was no broken skin, nor purpling.

"We've come to an understanding then," he said softly, tossed down the paddle and swung her up into his arms, cradling her on his lap.

She squirmed in his arms, pushing against his chest and scrambling off him. Dancing around the room she rubbed her bottom and protested, "Damn it, Hunter. That hurt beyond anything I've ever felt before!"

He slid his arms along the back of the sofa and sank back, crossing one ankle over his knee as he watched tears slide down her cheeks. "Yep, had to get a reaction. These people at the house —they'll know real from phony. So, next time, I'll go easy as long as you cry. You did well," he said. "But not too easy or they'll know I'm holding back when I shouldn't. Now, come sit down with me." He held out his hand to her.

All he could think of was having her sit close, her lush body against his with his arms around her.

Her sobbing had subsided and now she wore a disgruntled expression as she settled down beside him. He wound an arm around her shoulders and pulled her against his chest so he could reach her ass, which he rubbed with both hands. "It hurts," she complained again, though she remained in position.

He reached for a tissue in the box he'd placed earlier on the table.

"Yeah, it hurts, but it was necessary for the role you're playing."

"Believe me, next time I'll bawl my head off!" she exclaimed.

He grinned and shook his finger at her. "Uh-uh, remember, you need to be convincing to the House folks. The best thing I can do for both of us is to toughen up your ass."

He ached for her discomfort and sadness, loved her promises, but knew she'd be over his lap again sooner than later; it hadn't taken her long to start pouting again. He sighed. This was part of the training, and it was important she learn to show proper behavior as a submissive wife, and even if she obeyed him, he knew the pastor at the house would expect him to dish out maintenance punishment on a daily basis. Another item listed in the damned contract—which she hadn't read. Damn, the sooner they discovered his prey, and were out of that house the better.

Regina was an independent, modern day, strong-willed woman, and had her own ideas about living her life. But while she worked this job, she needed to give up that independence.

He provided comfort, as he would with any submissive with whom he'd done a scene in the past—providing her after-care.

But he frowned then at the thought of not having her under his thumb when the job was done, then shoved it away, surprising himself with the thought of marrying her. He'd had a wife, and it hadn't worked out for him—for them. Never again, he'd vowed. But then he thought, *but this is Regina. And Regina is nothing like my wife*. And as much as Regina wouldn't admit to it, he saw she emitted submissive tendencies. Which, to his mind, made her perfect for him. He guessed she didn't know she was a natural submissive, but his gut told him she was.

She eventually uncurled herself and he lifted her from his lap and set her on the couch. Rising to his feet, he swept a hand through his hair and started pacing. Paddling her over his lap had been too intimate; next time he'd do it over the back of the sofa, so it was less personal. But damn, he needed to have the intimacy since they needed to portray a loving couple. As he thought earlier, she was perfect for him. He couldn't see any reason why they couldn't pursue a relationship once this job was done.

He looked down at her where she sat silently on the couch, except for her sniffling, giving her a chance to recover. He hadn't meant to be so hard on her, but once he had her over his lap, he realized that's exactly where he wanted her. If she were his, she'd spend a lot of time in that position.

Books, he needed the books, to proceed because his mind had drawn a blank on how to. He found them on her bedside table and carried them into the living room. He sank down on the sofa beside her, his gaze traveling appreciatively over her huddled form.

Hardening his heart, he said, "We're going to look at these pictures and talk about the scenes as we may be called on to do some. They're typically used in the BDSM clubs throughout the country, and I guarantee we'll be doing some of these scenes at that house."

She hadn't replied, wouldn't look at him. Her face was buried against the back of the sofa. "Turn around, Regina," he ordered. "We need to get this down pat in the next two days."

CHAPTER NINE

Regina listened to him, knew he was right; this would be a crash course for her, though she knew he was far from being a novice on this BDSM crap like her. He was a natural. She'd always known and been attracted to Hunter's strong, dominant, personality though she'd never been on the receiving end of it, except on the job. He had years of experience so she'd always followed his lead.

Tired of huddling on the sofa, embarrassed by her near nudity, she lifted her chin, uncrossed her legs, and faced forward, cringing when her sore ass hit the cushion too hard. They had a job to do. Folding her hands on her lap, she left herself open to him.

Glancing sideways at her he nodded, his eyes ablaze. "Good start. Now spread your thighs."

Once again, heat tore through her body from head to toe, but she moved her legs apart.

"More," he instructed, turning to face her.

Her gaze took in his muscular torso again, and his tattoos and she gulped.

"Wider," he said. When she did, he whispered in her ear, "You've got it, babe. Now I'm going to touch you…"

He flipped through a few pages and pointed at a man

tweaking a woman's clitoris, her legs spread wide open, her head thrown back in arousal, "...like that."

Her eyes went wide, and she gulped, then whispered, "Okay, sir."

She'd call him sir, for she didn't want another trip over his knee, even though she knew it would happen again, especially since it was expected at that house. *Damn, what have I gotten myself into?*

Leaning over her, he settled his lips over hers, and she sighed when his tongue found its way inside her mouth. She jumped at the touch of his big hand on one thigh, then relaxed as he slid it back and forth over her skin as a prickling sensation took up residence in that area. Then he slid his hand to the inside of her thigh and pulled her leg outward, stretching her to her limits, leaving her completely exposed.

"Relax," he muttered, "lean your head back against the sofa. Remember now, we're supposed to be a married couple and madly in love."

Following his orders, she did, causing her body to slide forward a bit as she tried to relax, and closed her eyes. She jumped, startled at the touch of his big hand easily cupping her mound over her thong.

She heard him hiss, and her eyes opened to see his dark hair, his head looking down at the core of her, one finger circling her clit continuously, through the satiny fabric. Gasping, she stiffened and started closing her thighs again.

"Stop it," he ordered with a slap to her core and she gasped. Lifting his head, he looked into her eyes. "You need to accept my touch, in any way, any fashion. No stiffening up. Pretend I'm your loving husband, giving you pleasure."

Regina gulped. "It's...difficult."

"It doesn't have to be. I'm having no trouble touching you and trying to get you off, sweetheart," he drawled. "Just pretend, but do it convincingly or, better yet, wrap your mind around accepting and enjoying my touch and really get off."

She wasn't a virgin, but her problem was she'd never had a lover, or even a steady boyfriend for much more than a few months at a time, so had no point of reference about 'true love'. And she wasn't used to being nearly naked with a man without feeling self-conscious. Still, she was starved for physical gratification, she now realized, and thought, *what the hell*, why not get some enjoyment out of this?

"Yes, sir," she said as he dipped his head once more. She closed her eyes, heard a rustling noise, and frowned. Was he…undressing?

She felt his hand slide down to her hips and he murmured, "Lift your butt, sweetheart."

Frowning, she followed his orders, then gasped when he ripped her thong from her. Through astonished eyes she saw his head descend toward her stomach, then gasped when something warm, and wet flicked between her legs, at the center of her. Hunter had settled on the carpet kneeling between her thighs, his broad shoulders keeping them apart.

She had a strong hunch she was going to like what he planned on doing to her; no man had ever come down on her like this, yet she'd fantasized about it.

Her gaze roved over his smoothly muscled torso as she watched him lower his head to her.

"This is what's happening on the next page," he said. "Learn to enjoy my touch and this will all go smoothly."

He sucked her clit between his teeth and nibbled gently. Within an embarrassingly short few minutes, her body stiffened, and her eyes rolled back in her head as an intense climax rocketed through her. Once she recovered, she felt a hand unclench her fist, then open her fingers and kiss the palm of her hand. She opened her eyes and saw a satisfied look on Hunter's face as he knelt before her.

"You, babe, make me feel like the world's best lover." Shaking his head, he resumed his seat on the sofa next to her. "I think I broke my record for getting a woman off so fast." He chuckled then, his attention back on the book and he turned a page.

Narrowing her eyes, she asked, "Are you laughing at me, Monroe?"

He slid his gaze over her body, from her thighs to her eyes. Softly, he said, in a warning tone, "What did you call me?"

Prickles up her spine warned her she'd goofed up, yet she couldn't put up with his jocular attitude to her responsiveness—he didn't have to rub it in her face. Lifting her chin, she said, "Your name, that's what I called you."

He tossed the book on the end table and sighed as he came to his feet. "We're back to square one then. Was afraid this might happen."

She watched him quickly don his T-shirt.

"So we're done for the day?" she asked, hopeful.

He was pacing back and forth and finally stopped directly in front of her, snarling, "We are done. Period."

"What…what do you mean?" She knew exactly what he meant and cursed her inability to be a good actress. Everything had been fine until he'd gloated, but then, was his comment really gloating?

"I need to start looking for another partner."

She stood up and stretched her arms over her head, giving him an eyeful of her body, then she walked over to the island, shrugged into her robe and strode into the kitchen, giving her ass a healthy swing. To hell with him, she mused. He'd come begging to her again she knew, for what woman in her right mind would do what he wanted—expected—without a fuss. More coffee, that's what she needed. Thankfully, 'Sir' had made a full pot, so she poured herself another cup.

She watched him stuff the books in his bag, his glare on her the whole while she sipped her coffee.

"You're mad," she said.

He hiked the bag over his shoulder. "Disappointed. I truly believed, since we'd worked together so well in the past, this would work out."

"Woah, buster, never have we worked like this!" At his silence, she asked, "What will you do?"

He growled as he headed toward the door. "What I should have done in the first place. I know of several women at local clubs. One of them may work out."

She raised her brow. "Clubs?"

"Sex club, BDSM, yes."

Frowning, she said, "Then why hadn't you asked one of them in the first place instead of coming to me?"

His hand paused on the doorknob. "Because none of them have any police training. Later," he murmured as he walked out, closing the door behind him.

Anger encompassed her then as she looked at the door. He'd left her, after putting her through pain and ecstasy, he simply left her. She'd had every right to feel angry with him when he'd patted his back over his sexual accomplishments. *Getting her off*, my ass, she mused.

As she sank down onto a bar stool, coffee in front of her, she had nothing to worry about; she still had her job, though it would have been nice to have her credit card charges paid off.

The big question she had to ask herself, though, was why she couldn't do as he'd asked. Why had it been so difficult? They'd known each other for years, had worked together closely as partners. He'd always respected her as she did him, so what had been the problem?

She knew what the problem was—she had no idea what a Dominant-submissive relationship was all about. Had no idea about the BDSM world as she'd never experienced it. She also didn't have a submissive bone in her body—at least she thought she hadn't until Hunter had proved otherwise.

Regina could read books until she went blind on the topic, and it wouldn't help her learn a thing. Hunter physically making love to her made sense, but she simply couldn't get over their past history—they had a professional past. How could he expect her to leave that all behind and pretend they were married and lovers?

The bigger question in her mind was why had she submitted to him? Oh, sure, there was the reward of him paying off her credit cards and she admitted, a promotion would change her life at the station, but those weren't even in her mind while he spanked her. Yes, she'd protested, yes, it had hurt, but it also made her feel, dare she say it, loved? Safe and protected? But he'd ruined it for them with his gloating. The bastard.

CHAPTER TEN

Chicago

Hunter stalked into the The K Club, a private club located in Logan Square, and owned by Dorance Knight. He hadn't stepped foot in the place for over a year. After his last submissive relationship with Jeanine, which had lasted relatively long for him—three months—he hadn't wanted to return. At the time, he'd had it with submissives; they were a needy, jealous, possessive group, and he had to admit that that was one big reason he had always enjoyed being with Regina. Her strong-willed personality, while it begged for him to conquer her and make her submissive, made him also appreciate her strength and independence.

Settling onto a bar stool after checking in at the door, Knight happened to be behind the bar, and he strolled over.

"Man, haven't seen you in an age," he drawled. "How are things with the business?"

"Busy," Hunter said shortly.

Knight had been a good friend for several years, and never seemed to have a shortage of submissives interested in him. Though he was average in height and build, his friend's 'presence' commanded attention. He was somewhat aloof, his hair dirty blond, and he wore a steely-eyed expression that seemingly pierced through you. He emanated strength and confidence and personified 'Dom' in every way.

The bartender, one of Hunter's past submissives, hurried over. "So good to see you, sir!" she enthused.

Hunter had to stop himself from rolling his eyes. Damn, Tammy was her beautiful, blonde, curvaceous self—a sight for sore eyes, but she'd been the most possessive of them all with her whining, pouting and then causing a scene when he'd left her. He truly didn't expect such a friendly greeting as Knight had whipped her ass for making a scene in the club, then banned her for a month, but obviously, she'd gotten over it.

"Hey, Tammy. Black on the rocks, please."

She hurried away, and Hunter met Knight's raised brow.

"Starting out with the hard stuff, huh? You just looking or are you meeting up with someone?"

Hunter explained the job and situation and Knight whistled. "Damn, you've got your work cut out for you. I'm trying to think if there's anyone new here who might meet your needs. We've plenty of subs that could do the job, but none with any kind of defense or police training." He paused, and his eyes slid over Hunter's head. "Wait a minute, there is someone—maybe you know her." A chin jerk straight ahead and Hunter turned to see a tall, long-legged woman with straight to her waist black hair, and a lean figure strolling toward the bar. She wore a mask, however, and a black catsuit.

Hunter turned to Knight. "I don't recognize her, at least with the mask on I don't."

Leaning forward, Knight said, "You know we all respect confidentiality here, but this is an exception. That's Chief Maria Sanchez, from the Groveland Police Force," he murmured. "Isn't she something?"

Hunter gasped and choked on his last swallow, some spewing out of his mouth and onto the shiny bar's surface. *Gina's boss!*

Quickly, Knight swiped it up with a towel. "Get control, buddy."

"What the hell? Has she been a member for long? I've never seen her here before," Hunter said.

"About eight months now, once a week."

"No Dom yet has claimed her?"

Hunter caught Knight's posture straightening, an aloof look on his face as he replied, "No Dom, yet, though several have approached her. She's played with a handful, but nothing is jelling yet so maybe this is a good time to ask her."

Hunter looked steadily at his friend, realizing he had more than a passing interest in the chief. A slow grin crossed his face then. "You might be my life saver yet."

He stood up from his bar stool and strolled down to the opposite end. Luckily, there was a vacant stool right beside the chief. He stood behind her a moment, his gaze sweeping down her bare back to the crack in her ass. From the front, which had a modest neckline, one would never have known about the back side of the suit she wore. Olive-toned skin invited him to touch her, but he couldn't—wouldn't. He respected Chief Maria Sanchez too much.

Settling down beside her he took another swallow of his drink before turning and meeting her wide eyes.

"Hey, Chief."

He heard her gasp, smiled, and took another swallow.

"How did you know it was me?" she whispered.

"I'd recognize you anywhere, Catwoman." His grin widened. "Want to tell me why, when I told you about this job, you didn't volunteer yourself?"

"What would it look like if the community of Groveland knew...knew I...that I...well, was interested in this lifestyle? Also, there is the fact I am the chief of police and have a highly visible profile. The mayor would fire me in a heartbeat."

Staring at her wide-eyed expression, he guessed she was more than a little upset to have been discovered. He sighed. "No worries. I won't tell. And I see your point in why you can't do the job." Glancing around, he said, "Look over your right shoulder. Take a look at the guy in the black suit, white shirt and tie. Know who that is?"

She followed his directions, looked for the longest while but finally replied, "I saw him when I first arrived. He looks familiar, but I can't recall how I recognize him."

"Senator Thorn Thompson, from Iowa."

Marie Sanchez gasped. "But his hair color isn't…"

"Dye job of course. A lot of known, powerful men are members here and camouflage themselves in some way, in order not to be recognized. Including you."

She shook her head. "Damn, what is this world coming to?"

Grinning at each other, they chuckled companionably.

"Why are you here and not working with Officer Arrigoni?"

Hunter growled his reply. "There isn't a damned submissive bone in that woman's body, that's why. We tried, but speaking of not jelling…"

"Don't underestimate her," Sanchez interrupted. "She may surprise you yet."

"I don't have that much time. So," Hunter said, waving his arm around the club, "is this new to you?"

"Not new, just haven't been in the scene in a few years, until I found out about this place several months ago."

"How come?" At her surprised look, he added, "No worries, no need to say another word."

She shrugged. "I guess I could talk to you about it, seeing as you, apparently, are 'in the scene' as well."

"In and out—when time allows—in."

"You likely heard I moved here from Los Angeles two years ago."

"I had, yes."

"Well, I was—running I guess you could say."

Hunter raised his brow but didn't say a word.

She continued. "From a man, or rather I should say the memories of a man. Bad memories."

"Uh-huh," Hunter said, staring into her pretty, dark brown eyes. She was a strong, capable woman—one he could really use at the moment. He waited for her to continue, guessing what she had to share was tough for her.

"A man who nearly beat me to death."

Hunter gulped, stunned. "What happened? Was it—"

"—my Dom." She sighed. "The reason why I stayed away from the scene for that long. After I finally left the hospital I went to court, he was charged and imprisoned, and I left, hoping his sorry ass never got out of that prison. I've finally gotten up the courage to return to this world—I had to return you know? I can't ignore who I am, and I need a Dom—badly."

"Yes, I know what you mean, and I'm sorry that happened to you."

She cringed, and tears came to her eyes. "He had such a hold over me. Hell, I could have used my police training on him, but I didn't, I couldn't—I was too cowed by him, and I was angry at myself. I kept telling myself his abuse was normal, when obviously it wasn't."

"How long had you been his sub?"

"Five long years."

He gasped. "Right. I hear you." He patted her back carefully, not wanting to upset her more than she already was.

"That's why I went for the police chief job in Groveland—a small, bedroom community with practically zero crime." She smiled at him. "It's been the perfect job for me, and the perfect place. Believe me when I say it took a lot of guts for me to come into big city Chicago, seeking out another place for myself in a club. You see, I want to find that right 'Dom'."

"But you haven't met anyone yet?"

Maria lifted her chin and gazed down the bar. "Possibly."

Hunter followed her gaze to Knight standing behind the bar still, then smiled as he took another sip of his drink. He was glad to see his friend obviously had feelings for Maria as well. He frowned then, wondering why they hadn't tried each other yet. Some time he'd ask Knight.

He rose from the bar. "Take care, Chief Sanchez."

"Maria."

Hunter's grin widened. "Will do." He shook her hand and left her in solitude.

He sauntered down to Knight and sank onto the stool in front of him. "You've an admirer, did you know that?"

Was that a ruddy redness that appeared in Knight's cheeks?

"She's a goddess," he murmured, and added, "who has her choice of any Dom in this place. Why do you say she's into me?"

"All the while I was chatting with her, she seemed to only be looking down here—at you."

"You're wrong," Knight replied.

"Don't talk, just watch her for a while and see."

A short while later, Knight muttered, "Damn, you could be right."

"You going to approach her?"

"Absolutely. Once I figure out the right time."

"Do so very carefully, like a gentleman 'Dom' if you get what I mean. She's had a rough experience in her past."

Knight sucked in his breath. "Shit. Who?"

"I'll let her tell you about it."

Knight stared at Hunter for a minute then nodded. "Got it. Now let's get back to your problem."

"I'm open for anything you have to say."

"Bring your cop girl here."

Hunter scowled. "Why?"

"Regina is her name, right?" At Hunter's nod, he said, "She may be what I call a Kinesthetic learner."

Hunter set his glass down hard. "What in the hell is that?"

"Someone who learns by touch, experiencing things, and not by reading a manual or listening to a lecture."

"Hmm, you might be onto something," he murmured. Though he'd tried both ways—her reading the manual and him lecturing—then turning her over his knee, he explained. He also confessed how angry she was afterward.

Knight chuckled. "Think you may have confused her. Bring her here. Have her participate in a few scenes with you, me, or one of the other Doms, and I'll bet she'll learn faster than reading any damned book."

"I'll think about it, but I'm doubtful she'll go for it after what happened today."

"What did you do? Beat her ass for not calling you sir?"

Hunter groaned, and Knight threw his head back and

laughed. "You spanked her, huh? Bet that went over well. What did you use, that killer leather paddle?"

"I started with my hand, then switched to the leather. You know, once she got over her shyness at being bare-assed naked over my lap, she tolerated it. Not saying she liked it—but took it in stride. It's what happened afterward."

"What did you do?"

"Got her off in thirty-seconds flat, from the first touch. Damn, she went off like a rocket—like I've never seen a woman do. It was amazing. *She* was amazing..."

Knight shrugged. "Maybe she hasn't had any in a long while."

Frowning, Hunter said, "Yeah, maybe, but she was downright pissed, though it was my own damned fault for gloating about my sexual prowess."

"Yeah," Knight said as he tossed down the last of his beer, "I can see why that might piss her off."

CHAPTER ELEVEN

"**D**amn," Regina muttered. Somehow, her Visa amount had creeped up, so now she owed five-thousand total. Scowling, she searched her mind, knowing she hadn't used the card but then she sighed. She'd never qualified for a good interest rate so that compounded the interest. She must have missed a couple payments. She should have set up auto-pay but never did. "Damn," she said again as she closed the lid on her laptop. She had to take the job with Hunter after all if he even allowed her a chance again. If he didn't, she'd need to find a part time job, which would be tough since she worked rotating shifts on the police force.

And the only way she felt she could learn how to handle this job was to gain some first-hand experience. But how? Hadn't he tried to teach her? She could do it, she thought, if she didn't know the person with whom she was training. That was the problem; she'd been too close to Hunter, too self-conscious with him. She might be better off with a stranger; if she had success with someone she didn't know she could at least gain the experience she'd need, which would hopefully help her get over her shyness with Hunter.

Who was she kidding? She knew that wasn't the 'real' reason, knowing him so well as she did. Quite simply, her temper got the better of her at his gloating at getting her off. Why had she been so angry about that? Had she simply glommed on it as an excuse to get her out of the job she didn't really want to do? She needed a shrink to help her unravel her thoughts and feelings! Argh.

Suddenly, a name came to mind—Jillian Summers—the sluttiest girl in high school. Jillian had always been ready for a good time, and while she hadn't spoken with her since issuing her a speeding ticket when she'd worked on the Chicago Police Force a few years ago—she knew the woman had connections in deep, underground shit. Maybe she knew of a local club where she could watch, and participate even, to learn how to become a submissive, though she'd never felt she had a submissive bone in her body, but she could learn, especially when it came to the money. But then, she didn't know if Hunter would take her back, but it was worth a shot.

She found Jillian on Facebook and messaged her. Regina took a shower, dressed in shortie pjs, and when she returned to her computer was surprised to see Jillian had responded. After explaining the situation with Hunter, Jillian said she knew of several clubs in Chicago, but in particular spoke highly of one where she could learn a lot about being submissive in order to do the undercover job. She knew the owner and would put in a call.

———

Hunter watched Knight take out his cell, answering a call. After disconnecting, he settled it back in his pocket looking at Hunter.

"Well, this call was meant for you. It seems one of our members got a call from your ex-partner."

Scowling, he asked, "What the hell for?"

"Seems she's looking for a crash course on submissive training, hands-on experience, and one of our members gave her our name and location."

"Fuck!" Hunter snarled. "Knight, if Regina shows up don't let her in. She'd be like a babe lost in the woods."

Knight chuckled. "Isn't it ironic how we were just talking about this?"

"Yeah. Ironic, all right. Name of the member Regina contacted?"

"You know I can't divulge that information to you," Knight said dryly.

Tapping the bar with his glass, Hunter added, "Damn it. She was calm when I left, wasn't begging me, by any means, to keep her on." Something made her change her mind, he thought, then he grimaced.

"What?" Knight asked.

"I've a feeling she got her latest Visa bill. I told her if she did the job, I'd pay it off."

"Damn, how much, man?"

"Three k."

Knight growled, "If she were mine, she'd be over my knee, that's for sure."

"Yeah," Hunter replied, thinking he hadn't disciplined her yet for that one. "Can you find out when she'll be showing up? I think I've come up with an idea."

———

Regina found a parking spot on the street, just a few blocks away from the K Club. She parked, checked her bag for her police issued handgun, straightened her skintight, above the knee black skirt with a slit up one side, exposing a lot of thigh, and made sure the tails of her white, long-sleeved, button-down shirt were tucked in smoothly.

She'd opted for a pair of four-inch spike-heeled pumps in red —one of three pair Hunter had bought for her. She walked past shop windows, glancing at her reflection from the streetlights. *Darn!* She hadn't worn the skirt yet anywhere since she'd purchased. Luckily, the skirt was made of plenty of spandex, so it had lots of stretch.

She paused and looked at her side view in the window, hating her curvy ass—always had—genetics from her Italian mother. She'd endured the bubble butt all through high school and still wore the scars. Her hair she'd put up in a messy sort of bun, just to keep it out of her way since she had no idea what would transpire.

She sighed and walked to the end of the block where the club was located, though she couldn't find any sign. She'd been told she wouldn't see one, but to look for particular windows, doors and markings which she immediately found on the last store-front, at the corner. She tried the door, but it wouldn't open. That's right; the door would be locked the person who took her reservation said, so she had to knock—and not just any knock—but three taps, pause three taps again.

The door opened and a bruiser of a man with a bald head and arms like tree trunks stood there with a big-assed grin on his lips, one tooth gleaming gold. Jeez, she mused, just add a bandana to that bald head and he could man a pirate ship!

He looked her up and down closely and asked, "Your name, darlin'?"

"Reg—Reggie," she said.

He widened his stance and frowned down at the list in his hand. "Sorry, no one with that name has a reservation."

Darn. She'd forgotten she'd meant to give the person who took her reservation a false name and had given her real one instead. She sighed. "Regina Arrigoni."

The big guy's grin was back in place. "Now that one's here. You're in, sweetheart," he said as he crossed off her name and stepped aside to allow her to pass.

She walked forward but was stopped again by another giant. They could use some guys this size on the force. This one had long black hair tied in a low ponytail, bare-chested with unbeliev-able pecs.

"Good evening, ma'am. You can check your purse here," he said politely.

She shook her head. "The bag stays with me."

"No can do. No baggage of any kind allowed past this point."

Just then a couple other muscular guys walked past her with equipment bags over their shoulders. She pointed. "What about them?"

The guy nodded. "Those guys are Doms, and they can carry."

"Oh." Then she saw a tall woman go by, also carrying a big bag.

Pointing, she said, "What about her?"

"Also a Dom so she's good to carry."

"Huh." Learn something new every day. She didn't think about the possibility of a woman being a Dom. Grinning, she sorta liked that idea.

Comparing her manner of dress with the woman 'Dom', who wore a black silver trimmed corset and short black skirt exposing the lower half of her ass cheeks, her long red hair up in a high ponytail, she said, "Well, how do you know I'm not a Dom?"

His gaze ran up and down her figure. Cocking a hip to one side, he said, "First of all, it says here you were specifically asking for a Dom to teach you submissive practices. Second, you sure as hell don't look like any Dom to me, darlin'," he announced, leering suggestively at her. "You scream submissive."

Confused, she looked down at her clothing and shrugged, wondering what about her appeared submissive, especially since Hunter had complained about the fact she wasn't. While she hated leaving her purse behind, it appeared she had no choice, so she handed it over to him.

"Good girl," the guy said, and she felt heat fill her cheeks. "Don't move. I'll get your trainer."

Her cheeks still felt warm. Why a guy saying 'good girl' to her would make her feel all hot and bothered confused her. She looked around, checked out her surroundings.

The club was dark, as most clubs are, and it looked like a dance club-bar type of place. There was a fairly large dance floor where a DJ played music and several couples were bumping and grinding. A long bar ran around two sides of the dance area with black leather bar stools. The walls were painted black with an occasional splash of red splatter-painted on.

Moving further into the space, she saw a lounge type area with curved black leather sofas and coffee-type tables where several women sat with beverages. They were dressed to kill—rather dressed and on the hunt, Regina decided wryly, taking in the mini-skirts, shorts, midriff baring tops—some women were even topless, some had donned pasties. What? she mused. Was that even legal? She made a note to check the state statutes on it.

The black-haired ponytail guy came toward her, another man sauntering behind him. The new guy was tall but finely-muscled —no bulk. He wore black leather pants that laced up the front and hung low on his hips. Regina gulped as he stopped directly in front of her. He wore a long-sleeved black t-shirt fit close to his body, which surprised her since most men she'd noticed were bare-chested, except for body piercings and tattoos on them. His hair was longish in the front and dark, but she couldn't see his eyes as he wore a mask, reminding her of Zorro. Ponytailed guy made introductions.

"Regina, meet Jasper. He'll be your trainer."

"No shit," she breathed, looking him up and down.

"Regina, Jasper." And with that the man left.

Speaking of screaming, this guy screamed 'Dom' to her, big time. He seemed to be scowling down at her, then he took her hand without a word and pulled her past the bar area, and over to a private place with a leather couch and coffee table. In the stupid shoes she wore, she took four steps to his one.

"Kneel," he barked in a raspy tone.

"Uh, excuse me?"

"Are you hearing impaired?" he asked.

"No!"

"Kneel. Last time I'm asking."

Regina gulped and muttered, "You told, didn't ask."

"What was that?" he snapped as she started bending when he ordered, "Nix the shoes."

Glad he hadn't forced her to repeat her murmurs, she'd made the right choice not wearing pantyhose, so she toed off her shoes, and her feet and legs felt immediate relief.

Looking into his eyes, she slowly bent down, pulling up her skirt and maneuvering to her knees beside his. He looked at her passively, arms crossed over his smooth chest.

With a nod, he sank down on the sofa. "Generally, there is little talking in a club like this. I'm making an exception for you. Talk. Why are you here?"

"Why…I…I need to learn submission for…well, my boyfriend left me because I couldn't be. I want him back," she said, hoping he wouldn't detect the lie.

"Uh-huh."

Why did he sound skeptical?

He sank back on the couch, his eyes on her. Then, lifting one of his legs up and over her head, he trapped her between his knees. She shivered, wished she could see what he looked like behind the mask. For some reason, he seemed…familiar?

When she'd first arrived, she had noticed other men also donning masks, and wondered why. Perhaps they were public figures and didn't want their identities discovered.

"You don't learn submissive behavior. You either are submissive naturally or you're not."

"The man at the door said I was definitely—submissive."

"All right, then. Paul's excellent at making that determination."

"How can he when we just met?"

"He's been in the scene a long time and just knows."

Leaning forward, he took her hands in his and rubbed them. She felt like melting on the spot at his gentle touch. "Generally, before a newbie can even use the club, we have them complete some forms. But from what I hear, you insisted on no forms and that you had good reasons and the owner of the club agreed so I'll be asking some questions first."

At her nod, he continued. "What type of scenes have you participated in?"

She frowned. "Scenes?"

He waved his arm around. "Yes. Spanking, whipping, medical scenes, daddy-daughter scenes? Have you and your boyfriend done any of that? Have you ever been to a club before?"

She stuttered, "No club, and I've only been spanked a few times, but nothing else."

"Did you enjoy it? The spanking?"

"The circumstances were unusual, and I can't be positive, but I believe I did—enjoy it."

"What implement?"

"Excuse me?"

He sighed. "Were you spanked by a hand, a paddle, a whip? What?"

"It was a leather paddle, very whippy and stingy, and he also used his hand. I admit it hurt—a good hurt I guess." She bit her lip a moment, then added, "But I sorta put up a fuss about it so my boyfriend might have thought I didn't like it."

His silence unnerved her as he looked into her eyes, and relief flooded through her when he finally spoke again.

"So, let me ask you this. Do you enjoy inflicting punishment, on your boyfriend, for instance?"

She frowned. "I've never tried, but I don't think I'd enjoy it."

"Are you a pain slut?"

"No! Well, possibly, just not a lot of pain."

Leaning forward he looked deep into her eyes. "Has that boyfriend of yours ever taken you into subspace?"

"I—I don't understand what you mean."

"If you've simply been spanked with a paddle a few times, you likely haven't experienced subspace. We'll talk about that later, but for now, do you understand what it means to be submissive? Did your boyfriend explain it?"

"Sort of. He said I need to learn to obey his every word and command."

He nodded. "Sounds about right but know if a command is delivered and makes you uncomfortable, and you have to think twice about obeying, then you have the option to use a safe word."

She raised her eyebrows. "Oh, well, he didn't mention that."

CHAPTER TWELVE

Hunter dropped her hands, sank back against the sofa again, and mentally kicked himself. Damn, he'd spanked the hell out of her and forgot to mention choosing a safe word. But now that he thought about it, the pastor never mentioned the use of a safe word at the house, when there should be that option. Damn, how could he have forgotten something that important?

He had no idea of her pain tolerance and could have harmed her. This was one of the first things he'd learned as a Dom, and he'd fucked up. Giving himself some leeway since he'd been away from the scene for a while, he reminded himself to let whoever would do the job with him—Regina or someone else—to know, but he guessed since Regina had arrived for instruction, she'd changed her mind. Again. How she performed tonight would determine if she could do the job and if he'd take her back.

Leaning forward, he took her hands and, as he rose, pulled her up with him, then bent down, lifting each foot he replaced her shoes on her feet. He liked how she held onto his shoulders for balance. He rose, and now, standing face to face, he enjoyed how they were nearly the same height with her shoes on her feet.

"Shouldn't we talk some more?" she asked.

Shaking his head, he took her hand and pulled her along with him, passing the bar and making his way down a long hallway. "I have a feeling that you are submissive, but would appreciate privacy, so we're going to do a scene in a bedroom provided for that purpose."

He'd judged right as he pulled her into one of the larger rooms with a king-sized bed. Relief flooded her face, he noted, but then he questioned himself. If she decided to do the job, they might need to do scenes in front of other people at the house, which could be tough for her—the initiation, for one.

Today would have been their actual scheduled interview at the house, but he'd managed to plea illness for 'his wife', giving him time to find a submissive to take Regina's place. He was given a week's reprieve for their interview, so he had more time to work with the new girl, once he found her, but it looked like Regina had decided to live up to her promise to do the job, based simply on her being here now, and what she'd told him. Relief coursed through him.

He had no desire to have a wife along who couldn't defend herself, because his gut told him this house was trouble—big time. And Regina knew how to handle herself, thank God.

Yet, ironically, she hadn't tried to fight her way out when he'd disciplined her. It was human survival for someone to try and escape, fight for herself, but she hadn't, other than those few kicks and screams she gave over his knee, and that little dance she did after scrambling off his lap. So, maybe she truly didn't want to escape his punishment; maybe she enjoyed it.

He'd decided to don a mask, comb his hair differently plus adding a slightly red tint to it, and he made his voice raspy to conceal his identity from her. He'd also opted to keep on his shirt, knowing she'd seen his tats before and might recognize him. He had a feeling she'd been uncomfortable with him because they'd been partners, had been close to each other for two years, in a completely hands-off, professional manner. His disguise would hopefully rid her of her inhibitions with him.

Standing in the middle of the room, he turned on the dimmer switch, then proceeded to light several candles that had been placed around the room. Then he turned off the dimmer, leaving the room in a faint golden glow. This would be better for her, especially since he knew she was shy about her nudity. He'd gone about this all wrong with her back at her house and could have kicked himself in the ass for his lack of sensitivity. He'd made the mistake of thinking about Regina as the tough girl cop she'd been when they'd worked together, but was, in actuality, a shy, sexually inexperienced, woman.

He sat down on the bed, spread his legs, and locked his gaze on her. "While we're in here you will call me sir. Understand?" At her slow nod, he added, "Come here, girl. And remove the shoes again."

She didn't move. She looked like a deer frozen in headlights.

He snapped his fingers and pointed to the floor between his legs.

She hesitated a split second then kicked off her shoes before scurrying over on her bare feet.

"Kneel."

Quickly, she dropped to her knees and he nodded, satisfied.

"Service me," he growled as he leaned back on his elbows.

He decided giving her control at first might help her loosen up.

———

Oh, my God. I can do this. I want to do this.

Regina had dropped to the floor between his knees, licking her lips, her eyes focused on his groin. Reaching out, she managed to untie the lacing down the front of his pants, then carefully spread the gap open. Gazing down at him, she gulped. He was commando. God, what a delight! But then she narrowed her eyes, saw the glimpse of color on his lower torso, and moved the shirt aside.

Ohmygod, a tattoo—a familiar one. Hunter! Damn him! How dare he interfere. Question was how did he learn about her coming here to the club? She'd show him. She'd give him the best blowjob he ever had.

He was already hard, she noticed—and huge. Leaning forward, she licked the underside of his penis. She smiled to herself when she heard him catch his breath, and she continued licking him, sucking the tip, then she took him fully into her mouth. She held him in one hand as she sucked him in and out, and with the other, gently palmed his scrotum, occasionally squeezing and rubbing his cock up and down.

He dug his fingers into her hair and pulled. "Stop."

She immediately released him when she heard his pained tone of voice. She noted how he laid flat on the bed, his chest heaving, and he'd thrown an arm over his eyes.

She kneeled back but left one palm on his leather-clad thigh.

"Are you okay, sir?" she asked, smiling at her feigned worry.

He didn't reply at first, but after a while, he moved back onto his elbows, glared into her eyes, and hoarsely asked, "Who in the hell taught you how to do that?"

"I've parked a few times with boyfriends. I'm not a complete innocent," she said softly.

"I can see that…feel that. My turn now."

She rose to her feet. "But you didn't—"

"Not yet. We're taking our time here."

"Flat on the bed," he demanded as he rose to his feet.

She froze, recognizing *his* voice. It couldn't be! He didn't give her an opportunity to do any more thinking as he stood, grabbed her arm, and turned her to the side, giving her ass a wicked slap, refocusing her attention.

She started scrambling onto the tall bed when he leaned over, placed his hands around her waist and dragged her to her feet once more.

"Clothes off."

Regina heard the uncompromising tone in his order and decided not to question him and immediately shucked her skirt, and shirt, and placed them on a side chair beside the bed. She'd worn a red lacy bra and thong, her nicest set for this occasion, thinking they'd be perfect. By the heated look in his eyes, she thought right.

His gaze roamed her body from head to foot as he stood before her, his pants still unlaced, his hands on his hips. She wondered about his face beneath the mask and decided, if they really got into something hot and heavy, she'd reach up and snatch it off him. Wouldn't she love to see the look on his face once she revealed his identity.

She started to unclasp her bra but stopped when he said, "Leave the bra and panties on." He grinned then and added, "I like them."

She stood before him her hands folded at her waist.

"Bend over the foot of the bed."

Her breath caught at his command. Damn, was he going to spank her first? She was all geared up for some hot sex and instead, he wanted to punish her?

Biting her lower lip, her hands clenched, she asked, "Did I do something wrong, sir?"

"Move, Regina. Now."

"But why?"

"Because I am the Dom and give the orders, and you are the sub and follow them. Besides, you have no idea what I want to do to you, do you? There is something to be said about pain and pleasure being closely related. Are we on the same page now?"

He'd provided way more information than she expected him to give her. Was he one of those guys who could only get off after punishing his partner? She responded softly, "Yes, sir, but—"

A sharp slap landed on her ass again, this time beneath the curve of her ass where her thighs joined, and she shrieked and stumbled forward over the end of the bed.

"No more questions," he warned.

She closed her eyes as she lay on the bed, waiting stiffly for his next command.

"You said you've been spanked before. It just so happens that's one of my favorite past times."

Yep, she decided; he must be one of *those* guys... She braced herself as she heard him move around behind her. She knew because she lifted her head and looked directly into a mirror positioned above the headboard of the bed.

Darn it! The position afforded her the opportunity to watch him spank her and he'd be able to watch her facial expressions.

"You will open your eyes, brace your body on your forearms

and look into the mirror. Do not close your eyes and stay in that position. I want you to see me, and everything I do to you. Tell me your safe word."

She looked at him, confused.

"Why would I need—"

"In case you've reached your limits—if something I do is too much for you to handle. How about red? Always a good one. You say red, I stop. You say yellow, it means proceed cautiously."

"And green is a go, right?" she asked, with a slight smile on her lips.

He nodded.

She could remember this. Regina repositioned herself as he demanded. He moved away, and she lost sight of him in the mirror. But she heard his soft footsteps a distance away. Suddenly he appeared, a paddle similar to the one he'd used on her before in his strong grip. He didn't give her a chance to prepare herself when he pulled his arm back and came up with the paddle in an underhanded strike, right across her sit spot.

She cringed but managed to keep her composure.

"It's all right to cry or scream. No reason to keep it to yourself. Besides, screaming helps release endorphins. Keep your eyes on me now, in the mirror."

Her eyes widened when she saw him slip his fingers into the sides of her thong and slide it down just so far, at her mid-thighs, trapping her legs.

Then he began.

She did as he ordered, staring in the mirror and biting her lip and slap after slap rained down on her ass and thighs. She flinched with each slap but kept her complaints to a minimum. Maybe it was because he appeared to be doing a dance around her body, striking her hard, then soft, muscles flexing as he moved around her with the wicked paddle, gauging her body, smoothing the skin of her ass in between smacks. Truth be told, she was mesmerized by this erotic dance he performed.

Frowning then, her body jolting forward from his next slap, she wondered why she'd protested his treatment at her house. She had to wonder about her feelings then. While she'd felt humiliated the first time Hunter had spanked her, now she felt a welcome heat in her lower extremities, a growing wetness between her thighs, and a tingling there as well. How perverse, she decided.

His chest gleamed with sweat, his muscles bulging whenever he slapped her. Then he spanked her sit spot repeatedly until she moaned, as a combination of exquisite pain and pleasure mixed together. Her mind drifted away, and she closed her eyes. She'd lost count and didn't care. The unexpected, wondrous sensations rippled through her body, in between the pain, until the pain was almost non-existent, and she felt nothing but pure pleasure.

"Girl," he growled. *Smack. Smack.* "Open your eyes and look at me."

Her eyes popped open when she felt his hand at her waist. She smiled at his somewhat worried expression. "I...I think I'm floating," she whispered, unable to keep her eyes open.

He continued where he'd left off, fingered her clit every few slaps and she gasped, and her eyes closed again as she whispered, "Yes, yes!"

———

She was floating she'd said—subspace. She was into it, he realized as he fingered her toward climax. He allowed her, this time, to keep her eyes closed. Never had he been able to spank a woman to orgasm, though he'd tried—sometimes because he wanted to —sometimes when his current sub asked him to. This time he knew he'd succeeded because it was Regina.

His finger slid around and over her clit, the surface slippery and wet as he felt it expand beneath his touch. He recognized when a woman was right on the edge, ready to go over, and just when he sensed this in Regina, he snatched up the leather and delivered several light slaps to her ass again, grazing the soft tissues surrounding her clit with the other hand, pleased when she came, her screams like music to his ears.

He dropped the paddle to the floor and found a warm fleece blanket over the back of a leather chair, draped it over her, then he picked her up and placed her on the middle of the bed. Lowering down beside her, he covered her completely with the blanket. She didn't move. She lay flat on her stomach, her arms crushing a pillow, eyes closed.

He massaged her back and shoulders and when he heard her gentle breathing, he smiled. She had fallen asleep, even though he'd put her through some tough paces. Glancing at his watch, he saw it was eleven. He'd let her sleep a bit, then escort her to her car. But he wouldn't allow her to drive. He would drive her home, stay with her, not wanting to take any chances on what state of mind she would be in when she woke up. Besides, he knew he should reveal his identity to her as well.

Turning onto his side he faced her, and stroked her hair off her forehead—beautiful, bountiful, dark but streaked with red, then he closed his eyes.

Sometime later, he awakened at the feel of wetness between his legs. Groggily, he opened his eyes to find Regina kneeling over him, at his feet, giving him a blowjob—finishing what she'd started earlier.

He went to sit up and she snapped, "Stay. Your turn now."

Hunter stayed put, though he'd have to talk to her about topping from the bottom, giving him orders. He didn't like it—had a few subs that also tried—but they hadn't lasted in the relationship. He was the top—always. He'd enjoy her ministrations now since he hadn't gotten off yet.

Admittedly, the girl knew how to give a blowjob. She'd brought him close three times, but each time, using his tantric training, he was able to stop himself from climaxing, bringing that energy back inside him. He decided when he'd come, not her.

She'd been at it for twenty minutes until she leaned back on her heels and glared at him.

"Why won't you come?" she snarled, "sir!" she added with little respect in her tone of voice.

CHAPTER THIRTEEN

I t took all of his self-control not to laugh outright at her exasperation.

Lazily, he sat up, came to his feet, looking down at her with his brow raised. She started to stand, and he snapped, "Stay there, girl."

She'd taken him seriously, which was a good thing, and had stayed kneeling at his feet. As he laced up the front of his leather pants, he thought about the Regina he'd always known, and realized why she was angry. She was a woman who loved gaining the upper hand over her fellow cops—had tried with him several times, but never achieved it, except at the gym but then she'd slipped. It had been an accident. No woman got the upper hand on him.

Then he thought back to the arguments they'd had while working together. Remembered how she'd back down and always allow him his way when he threw around the fact he'd been a cop a hell of a lot longer than she had. Same could be said now; he'd been a Dom a long time, while she was just learning about submission and the rules.

When he was done lacing up his pants, he reached down. "Take my hand."

She paused a half a second then clasped it and he raised her to her feet. Looking at her without her shoes, she was shorter than him by at least four inches and, reaching up he pushed a hank of her hair behind her ear.

"Get dressed."

"No, I need to do another scene, something different than spanking," she said. "Sir, please, I need to learn more, my boyfriend said. Give me some different commands and I'll follow your orders—that's what he wants." Then she mumbled, but he heard her say, "Also, it helps me learn to be confident with myself —my body—being naked, helpless—you know."

"Your boyfriend can stick it up his fucking ass. You've been through a lot tonight, even went into subspace—have him explain *that* to you," he grumbled. "I'm driving you home. Now."

He helped her dress, and she didn't say another word but stared at him closely. Just when she'd put her shoes back on, she reached up and surprised him when she yanked his mask off.

"I knew it was you," she snapped. "What in the hell are you doing here?"

He growled, "You just had to know, didn't you?"

She shrugged. "Actually, I had an idea it was you, not right from the start, but after we came back here, when you unlaced your pants—I saw the tattoo." Narrowing her eyes, she asked, "How did you know I was coming here?"

He'd jammed his hands on his hips and now looked down on her, trying to intimidate her with his 'Dom' expression, but she wasn't buying it. He heaved an irritated sigh. "Have you forgotten your place?"

She growled back, "We're out of character right now. No acting. Be honest with me!"

He sighed. "I'm good friends with the owner. A friend of a friend of ours heard about you calling, and when I came in looking for a sub to take your place, I was told you'd reserved yourself a dominant for training. The big question I have for you is why in the hell did you come here? And don't tell me about the fictional boyfriend wanting you to learn to be a sub."

"That fictional boyfriend is you. I went online to my two credit cards and saw I owed more money than I thought," she muttered.

He rolled his eyes and cursed under his breath, watching her standing before him, biting her lower lip. Then he caught the pleading look in her eyes.

"I need the money. Please, Hunter. I know I'll be able to do the job. I did okay tonight, here, with you, didn't I?"

"Damn, woman, you need to get control of your finances," he groused. "And this is it. I'll take you back, but no balking at orders. Got it?"

She grinned. "Yep, I'm ready," she said enthusiastically. "And you're just the ma—Dom that can help me with that, can't you, *sir*?"

He paced the floor awhile, took her arm then, and without a word, pulled her out of the room, down the hallway and out the door, a chorus of "See you later, Hunter," following in his wake.

"And no being sensitive about my comments to you about your lack of experience," he added. "Your innocence. That's what left us splitting in the first place."

"You didn't need to be so nasty, saying what you did about me—to me..."

"Coming?" he snapped.

"Yes!"

He sighed. "You're right. I shouldn't have said it but damn, woman, you made me feel like—"

"—a man who knows what a woman wants. What a woman needs," she said softly.

His heart skipped a beat at her comment. He opened his mouth, ready to reply but stopped since he had no idea how to respond to her compliment.

She stumbled along behind him and then he came to an abrupt stop at the curb.

"Where are you parked?"

"About a block down." She pointed down the street.

Again, he pulled her along as she tripped behind him in her high heels. He knew her car and when he saw it, he stopped at the passenger door and held out his hand. "Key, girl."

Gritting her teeth, she said, as she handed him her keys,

"What's with this girl stuff? I heard some Dom calling another girl that. And the guy that checked me in called me that also."

"Just what we call our subs."

"I have a name!" she snapped.

"To me you are girl or wife, until after this job's done. And I am sir, remember."

He unlocked the door. "Get in."

She narrowed her eyes on him. "This is my car, sir."

On her muttered 'sir' she yelped because he'd slapped her ass.

"Stop pushing me," he said between gritted teeth. "I'm driving."

Rubbing her sore ass a moment, she groaned as she sank down into the passenger seat and folded her arms across her chest.

He choked back laughter when he saw the pout on her lips. "Seatbelt," he reminded her.

She nearly ripped the belt out of the car yanking it on. Satisfied, he closed the door and went around to the driver side, slid in, locked the doors, and started the engine.

"Why do you feel you need to drive me home?"

He glanced over, saw her face was red with suppressed anger and grinned before replying.

"You reached what's called subspace, where you could become dizzy, spacey—you had a floating feeling, you said."

"I remember that," she murmured, "but have no idea why that happened."

"It happens upon the release of endorphins when the body experiences stress—like the spanking I gave you. I managed to bring you back though when I started touching your clit, bringing you to orgasm."

She smiled. "Yes, that was—lovely."

He rolled his eyes, smiled, and patted her knee. "You need to get some rest. I didn't want you driving tired. And tomorrow is a new day."

She gasped then. "Isn't the interview tomorrow?"

"I managed to get us an extension, so we can train another week before the interview."

"I can do it," she said firmly. "After tonight, I know I can."

———

The following week flew by. Hunter worked her hard, demanded more than he ever had from any sub he'd been with in the past. She did well, followed every order. And because of it he spent less time disciplining her and more time rewarding her—with orgasm after orgasm. There was just one thing left to do, and he'd been putting it off, because it was so intimate—too intimate—and he didn't know if Regina would do it.

He decided he'd wine and dine her at a special place this evening. Then when they returned to her home, he'd talk to her about making love to her. They'd done plenty of foreplay, had plenty of orgasms—both of them—but he'd never penetrated her, not that he didn't want to. But they could practice doing it without him actually 'doing it', by engaging in typical mission position. He'd learned from the informant that there were cameras planted in every private and public space, including all of the bedrooms but not the bathrooms. That room was where they'd need to spend a lot of time.

He could cover her, and the cameras wouldn't be able to pick up much except for his naked backside.

They'd just finished their final session. Regina was as ready as she'd ever be. Now he paced her living room, waiting for her while she dressed. He'd already showered and dressed in the guest room and bathroom across the hall from her. As he'd left his room, he caught glimpses of her through her slightly open door, his gaze riveted on her as she undressed and left the bedroom for the shower.

That's when he strode down the steps, poured himself a scotch and sank down on her comfortable sofa.

Soon he heard her high heeled feet running down the steps, and he rose and set down his glass on the coffee table. He looked over his shoulder and gazed at the beauty before him.

Red, she wore red, and damn, he liked her in red. It was a halter dress, exposing a fair amount of the creamy skin of her breasts. Her arms and shoulders were bare, the skirt was full and of some kind of light, gauzy material that skimmed her knees. He gulped when he ran his gaze up her sleek, bare legs, then landed on the red stilettos on her feet. He stopped himself from tilting his head back and howling like a wolf.

"You like, sir?" she asked as she stood in the entrance to her living room.

He knew he wore a wolfish grin. "I like. A lot."

He strode over to her, then tweaked a long curl back over her shoulder. "You look lovely, and I'm proud to be seen with you. But I've a favor to ask tonight," he softly added.

"Oh? What?"

"No 'sir' tonight. Just Hunter, if you don't mind."

Shaking her head, she moved to a closet and removed a silky shawl. "Nope, have to, sir. Or I'll forget it once we get to that house, and I am going to try and avoid an ass blistering, if I can," she said cheekily.

He wound an arm around her waist and pulled her against him. "All right, but remember what I said about in public, though."

"I remember. I've a suggestion," she said softly. "Why don't you order for me? I'm afraid I'll slip with the 'sir' with the waitress standing there, I'm so used to saying it now."

"That was the plan since I know what you like."

His heart pounded, his cock pumped painfully as he escorted her out the door, took her key and locked it. Then he escorted her to his car.

Damn, she was becoming more submissive than he'd ever thought she would, and it gave him pause. Frowning as he opened the passenger door and she climbed into his car, he hoped to God she hadn't gone overboard on the submissiveness and remembered her police training. She needed to be on her toes once they got inside the house. He should have had one more gym session with her, but it was too late now.

CHAPTER FOURTEEN

Regina covertly glanced at Hunter as he shifted his car into drive, thinking he looked good enough to eat. He wore a black suit, cut close to his strong, lean-muscled frame, with a white shirt and a patterned red and black tie. She looked down and noticed the cufflinks in his cuffs and grinned to herself. Figures. Black onyx, a perfect foil against the white shirt. She didn't think she'd ever seen him dressed so elegantly, which made her wonder about the occasion. She noticed his hands, big, strong, yet elegant, a signet ring of gold with his initials embedded on it. She knew the ring—knew he always wore it. He'd explained once upon her asking about it and his reply was that all men in his family were given one upon their sixteenth birthdays.

They'd completed a lot over the past week, but she knew he had something on his mind. She knew him well since they'd been partners, knew when he grew quiet, he was thinking, but what could it be she wondered?

She felt confident in the training she'd had and knew she could perform the job to his satisfaction, yet something was off. He seemed, well, nervous…in a way.

The valet parked Hunter's car as he escorted her into the Tres Chic French restaurant. She'd never been there, had always wanted to, but never had that kind of money to pay for a dinner, and no escort. She sank into the softest leather bench seat and rested her elbows on the granite topped booth.

"Scoot in, sweetheart," Hunter said, motioning with his hand.

A warmth filled her when he sank into the seat right beside her instead of sitting across from her. He unwound the shawl from around her shoulders, folded it, rose and set it on the seat across from them, then sank down beside her again.

Grinning at him, she said, "Did I forget to mention you look wonderful, sir?" she said softly.

He chuckled. "I saw the look in your eyes and knew you liked what you saw."

"I did, I do. I don't think I've ever seen you so dressed up before."

"Don't do it much, at least not lately." He turned to her then and said, completely off subject, she noted, "We need to touch base on something we should have talked about earlier. There's one more important step we need to take, something I have yet to cover with you."

"Oooohhh, so you were naughty and forgot something important? Does that mean that I get to—"

"Regina," he warned.

"—spank *you*?" she said daringly, her eyes twinkling.

He glared at her and she sighed. "So much for wishful thinking. Anyway…" She shrugged, and added, "You seemed quiet, so I knew something was up." Biting her lip, she gave him a hesitant look. "Have I done something wrong? Something that needs correcting before we go to the house tomorrow, sir?"

He sighed, took her hand, and gently rubbed her knuckles. "No, you've learned well, have done everything right."

"What's left then?"

"We need to, tonight, we need to…" He slicked his hair off his forehead, and she noticed the uncomfortable look on his face. It had to be the worst of the worse, she decided, since he didn't know how to tell her. But what else could there be? He'd humiliated her, spanked her; he'd done things to her she would never allow any other human being, all for the job of course. She sighed internally. Who was she kidding? She wanted this man in her life —permanently—and would do just about anything to have him. Then she wondered what was left for her to learn to complete this job, then realized there was one thing more. Sex.

"What's wrong?" she asked again.

The waitress appeared then, a pretty blonde woman who couldn't keep her eyes off Hunter.

Regina glared at her, but softened her expression when Hunter glanced at her. She didn't want to get disciplined this evening, since tomorrow would be their big day and he'd be doing that enough as it is.

Once he placed their order of a chateaubriand dinner for two with a fine bottle of wine, he wound an arm around her waist, dipped his lips to hers and kissed her.

She sighed blissfully at the pressure of his lips against hers and wound her arms around his neck. This part of the training she definitely enjoyed.

After too short a time he broke the kiss and leaned his forehead against hers. "I don't know how to even approach this— subject with you."

She heard the tentative tone in his voice and frowned, thinking she'd never heard him talk with so little conviction.

The untimely appearance of the waitress with their wine made them part, as the woman went through the ritual of Hunter examining the label, tasting the wine and approving it, then she poured them half a glass each, and left. Finally.

He tipped his head back, took a long couple gulps of wine, then looked at her. "We need to have intercourse."

Regina gasped, then her heart started racing. She wondered why he'd never gone the whole way and made love to her. He was always holding himself back, even though he'd always left her satisfied. And she'd reciprocated. Still, she wondered...and now she knew why; he was worried she'd turn him down? *Hell no! He might be playacting, but she wasn't. She'd wanted to jump him from the first time she met him.*

Yet, she played it cool. "Why do we need to do that?" She kept herself in check, but what she wanted to do was jump him, drag him out of the restaurant and home where she had fantasies of tying him to her bed. Which he'd never allow, but then she smiled with the thought of him tying her up…

"We're a married couple, remember? Which reminds me…"

She watched him dig around in his jacket pocket, then produce a black velvet box. She gasped when he opened it, and without giving her a chance to gawk, he slid a solitary round cushion-cut diamond engagement ring and diamond-studded wedding band on the third finger of her left hand.

"There," he said, smiling into her eyes. "Now you look like a married woman."

Tears filled her eyes as she looked at the rings. "Are these for real, sir?"

"Yep. Though once I explained to the store manager that what I wanted was to rent not buy them, he was fine with that."

Regina examined her feelings. Why did his words sadden her? Her eyes glimmered with tears as she looked down at her hand and sighed. She loved the ring set, and it would be difficult giving them back.

At that moment, their food arrived. The waitress set down a large platter filled with the steak in the center, piped, buttery mashed potatoes circled the meat, with a mound of asparagus on each end. Regina's mouth watered, but not enough to stop their conversation.

"With that said, let's eat," he said heartily.

Her mouth gaped, and her eyes widened. "Wait a minute, you can't just drop something like that on me and then not say another word about it!"

He shrugged as he cut a portion of meat and placed it on her plate. "Why not? You heard me."

"Why?" she snapped.

Slowly, he placed the knife and fork down on the edge of his plate. "Because-I-say-so."

Regina just knew if they weren't in a public place, he'd have her over his knee, and after each word a swat would follow on her ass.

"Is that a fact?" she asked, reining in her anger.

His eyes glinted down at her. "Yes, it is." He sighed then took her hand. "We need to behave, in every way, as a husband and wife, because, well, I've learned the rooms have cameras in them."

She pulled her hand from his. "You have got to be kidding."

"Wish I was. You can't be surprised about it, right?"

"I guess not." Heat soared through her body at the idea of them making love and she shrugged. "I suppose you're right," she said vaguely, trying to appear cool, calm, and collected when she was anything but. Her core was hot, wet and ready to go at it with him. She couldn't wait until they arrived home, so she started eating more quickly.

Then she glanced sideways at him, saw him chewing his food industriously, gulping wine in between, and she smiled to herself. Was it possible he was nervous about it? She wasn't, and it was about damned time as she'd been wanting to jump him since the first orgasm he'd easily pulled from her.

With his mouth half full, he said, waving his fork a bit, "No worries, though. I've come up with an alternative solution."

Regina's spirits fell as she thought, what other solution could there possibly be besides having full-fledged intercourse.

"We're acting, and we've become good at it. What I'll do is simply cover you."

She dropped her fork and it clattered on the table as she leaned forward. "Cover me? What the hell does that mean?"

"That means my body's bigger than yours, and I can lay on top of you and mimic intercourse."

With that said, she had no response. None at all.

CHAPTER FIFTEEN

The drive home was tense, with unsaid words, and Hunter knew he was the one to blame. But then again, he'd told her exactly what he expected—it was part of her job—and he'd be paying her big time on those damned cards. She owed him, including the forgotten discipline she deserved because of those over-extended cards.

He couldn't figure out her coolness toward him, though, when he told her he'd 'cover' her. You'd think she'd be happy about it, considering how shocked she'd been when he'd first told her they had to have intercourse. But then, he hadn't missed the gleam in her eyes at his words…and then the droop in her visage when he said they'd fake it. It was almost as though she'd been disappointed? Impossible. Damn, but the woman confused him.

They arrived at her house, walked up the sidewalk, Hunter following her smooth, long strides as he admired her legs. Lovely legs, lovely breasts—sweet ass—what the hell—she was perfect.

He moved in front of her as he had her key and unlocked the door. She gave him a small smile as she went inside, removed her shawl, hung it back up in the closet, then turned to him. "I'm going to bed. See you there."

Hunter watched her hips swing as she strode into her room, leaving the door open for him. Damn, he wanted her, more than he'd ever wanted any other woman—even his ex-wife—yet knew he couldn't just take her.

Or could he?

He yanked off his suit jacket, hung it in the guest room alongside his other clothing, then showered and brushed his teeth. As he stood next to the bed, he frowned, wondering how he should dress—or undress.

It was too hot for a robe, yet he knew he couldn't just walk into her room nude. He opted to leave on his black jockey briefs and then, before leaving, he remembered an important thing. Rummaging in his suitcase he found the package of condoms he always carried with him. But he couldn't recall when he'd last used one, so he narrowed his eyes on the date and sighed in relief. They weren't past expiration, but close.

They would be mimicking intercourse, but he wasn't taking any chances and would wear one since he'd be right on top of her.

Clutching them he strode down the hall and entered her bedroom just as she came out of the bathroom with a white fluffy towel wound around her body.

"I'm ready," she said softly.

What the hell? Was that a tremble he heard in her voice?

He stopped in his stride, in the middle of the bedroom. "Drop the towel."

His heart raced when she obeyed him.

She stood in front of him, completely nude, arms at her sides, meeting his gaze.

He strode to meet her. He wound his hands around either side of her face and pulled her to him, kissing her lips until she sagged against him. He released her then, planted a hand on her sternum and gave her a little shove. She ended up flat on the bed, a surprised look on her face.

"I can do this," she said, with a nod and a smile on her face. "Since we're faking it, I can do this."

That gave him pause and he scowled at her. Damn, so she was happy they were faking it? Well, of course she was. They were working together; they weren't involved with each other. He sighed. But damn it, he'd like to be. He soured at her happy expression. She couldn't have made him feel lower than he felt right now. Faking it. Damn…

Hunter stood beside the bed, staring at the most beautiful woman he'd ever seen, stark naked, waiting for him to fake intercourse.

He turned away, tried to think how to proceed, still clutching the condom. He was the 'Dom', her sir. Why was he hesitant? He had no reason to be. This was a job that needed to be done. Period.

"Come to bed, Hunter. It's late, and we have an early afternoon interview tomorrow, don't we?"

"Uh-huh." He dropped his shorts and they fell to the floor.

He turned his back to her, tried sliding on the condom, but his hands wouldn't cooperate.

"Need help with that, big guy?"

He glared over his shoulder and found her smiling at him.

"What did you call me?"

Her smile widened. "Sir?"

"Uh-huh." *Payback was in order.* "Yeah, nice of you to offer." He climbed over her prone body, straddling her stomach and handed over the condom.

Her hands shook—he saw it and satisfaction was his. She was nervous.

"Why, if we're faking it, are you wearing a condom?" she inquired, staring at him as she rolled it down over his cock.

Damn, he was hard as stone and so ready for her.

"In case I can't control myself." He looked into her eyes. "Being responsible here. Wouldn't want an unwanted pregnancy."

"Ah," she choked, "thanks for that."

He wondered at the sadness in her eyes when she looked up at him.

"Okay." He sank back on his haunches, still straddling her, looking down at his hard cock in chagrin. "Since I'm on top, and we'll be in this position each night at the house, I'll be controlling the action."

One fine eyebrow arched inquisitively. "So, we are going to have some 'action' then?"

He narrowed his eyes. "You know what I mean."

"But there's no reason why I can't be on top, is there?"

"I'm the Dom. How many times do I have to tell you that I control the situation, not you, my sweet submissive. You need to stop talking so much," he growled.

"Just jokin'," she muttered.

"For tonight, we'll try this a few times, to get the feel of it. You need to pretend like you're enjoying it as the camera will be on your face," he warned.

"And on your backside," she reminded him cheekily.

He leaned back further, flipped her to her side and slapped her ass.

"Ouch!" she protested, wriggling to flip onto her back, but he held her on her side.

"Any more smart-ass words?" he asked, his big hand raised. His gaze landed on her ass and just one slap had her cheeks turning pink. Virgin skin, damn, he mused. He'd have to go easy on her once they were inside the 'house'. His gaze met her eyes then and she'd tightened her lips, kept her mouth shut. Her brow was furrowed, though. She shook her head, scowling at him.

"Fuck the scowl and give me the sweet submissive look I need, darlin'."

She widened her lips, showed her teeth, her eyes round like saucers. He rolled his eyes, allowing her to lay down on her back again.

He remembered the informant telling him, besides cameras, there were mirrors all over the building. "Wiseass," he grumbled then sank down on her, his groin flush against hers. Damn, her skin was softly rounded and hot—so hot. Groaning, he closed his eyes as he wound his fingers through the hair on either side of her head, dipped his head and kissed her lips. Kissing her simmered his insides but revved up his cock. He tore his lips away from hers then pressed down with more weight on her body; he couldn't miss her gasp, followed by her own little mewling noises and he raised up and sank back on his knees once more, straddling her waist.

"Did I hurt you?"

Her eyes were closed, and she shook her head. "No. It just feels…so…goo…uh, okay." She opened her eyes and added, "Can I put my arms around you?"

"You damned well better. We want this to look real."

Relief flooded him when she wound her arms around his waistline. Sweat spread across his forehead and chest and his cock sprang up to his belly button as he sank down on her again. "I'm going to mimic this now."

"Yep," she whispered, "and don't worry, I can take it, as hard as you want to deliver it." She'd closed her eyes again, kept her mouth open as she breathed in and out, her arms still holding him.

His heartbeat picked up at her words, even as his cock slid between her folds. She gasped, and he started to change his position when she murmured, "That feels so good. You can…keep it there and just start moving, faster," she encouraged him.

"You're topping from the bottom, Regina. Stop it," he growled.

"Sorry," she whispered.

"Spread your legs wide apart," he ordered, then added, "let me know if this hurts at all, if my weight is too much for you."

"I don't think that'll be a problem." She peeked one eye open and smiled at him as she spread her legs.

"All right, then," he said, and he rose up on his knees, then pressed his groin against hers a couple times, stopped, then back on his knees once more. His hands he'd splayed on either side of her body, near her shoulders. Staring down at her, her eyes were still closed but she had a grin on her face. "You enjoying yourself?"

"Oh, yeah," she breathed, as he pushed forward again. He did a bump and grind against her several times when he heard her breathing quicken. Reaching up, he tweaked one nipple, then the other, and he couldn't remove his gaze from the sight of her beautiful nipples budding hard beneath his fingers.

She groaned and arched her body after he removed his fingers, as if she was seeking attention once more. He returned to rolling them until they hardened sweetly again.

Then his breathing increased. Damn, she felt so good, even just this simple rubbing and grinding had made him harder.

He pressed down, put more weight on her, and she raised her hips, arching up against him. He ground against her more, his breathing growing shallower, but he paused when she spoke again.

"Let's just do it, sir. Please, just…"

She'd given him the green light and he took advantage of it and easily slid inside her. She was wet—she was heaven, and all thought left his mind except taking her.

He plunged in, then out, over and over, until they were gasping, their heartbeats pounding as they reached…reached, then he raised himself up slightly, shoved his hand between their bodies, then rubbed his thumb on her clit.

Groaning, heaving, he felt Regina raise her long limbs around his waist and lock her ankles behind his back. He heard her gasping, breathing faster and knew she was close to having an orgasm.

With just a few more hard strokes she came, tightening around him, biting her lip. He pressed his lips against hers, preventing her from biting so she couldn't hurt herself, then he stiffened, and growled, "Fuck," as his cock pulsed, pumping his seed inside the condom, then seemingly more and more he released until he was spent. When he was through, he rolled away and lay beside her, arms above his head, until he felt her nudge against his side. Gathering her in his arms, he held her pressed against his chest as they both calmed their ragged breathing.

Soon they quieted, but he didn't release her even when she went to move away. And he had no idea what to say about what had just happened. She solved the problem for them, in her straightforward manner.

"Um, I think we…did it?" she murmured softly, then nuzzled his earlobe.

He grinned. "Ya think? We did. You gave me the go-ahead. You okay, subbie?" he asked, his arms still around her.

"You mean wifie," she said.

"That too." Turning his head, he planted a deep kiss on her lips.

He planned on sleeping with her tonight, in her bed, holding her. There was no way in hell he'd return to the guestroom. As far as he was concerned, they belonged together, and this was no longer a job. Once the job was completed, he'd marry her. She'd want to. He knew Regina wasn't a swinger, but an old-fashioned Italian girl. She'd want marriage. He hadn't missed how her eyes had misted over when he'd given her the rings, as though it was all real. Still, it was too soon. They were just beginning.

"So are you okay with this?"

"Yes. No regrets. I've wanted to be with you like this for a long while," she whispered.

He looked deep into her eyes. "You have?" At her nod, he said, "Then why so coy?"

"Well, since you came, I had initially thought you were married. Once I found out you weren't any longer, I still thought I'd better not take the initiative since you're the Dom, and I didn't want to get spanked again," she added dryly.

Grimacing, he said, "I most likely would have, too." Then, in a hard voice, he said, "and you would have deserved it."

She sighed. "I'm used to going after what I want. And this is merely acting. Once we're done with the jobs won't things change between us?"

Leaning up on an elbow he stared down into her big brown eyes. "You do know I am truly a dominant, right?"

Her big brown eyes got bigger. "Not really...you are?"

He laughed at the confusion in her voice. "Yep, though I've not had a sub in quite a while. But now that we're in this relationship, I lead, and you follow."

She raised her brow. "*Are* we, in a relationship? For real?"

He scowled. "What do you think?"

"I think you're right." Her mouth turned up into the biggest smile as she sat up and sprawled across his chest, forcing him to lay flat on the bed. Taking his head between her hands, she kissed him until his cock came alive again.

"Wait, darlin'," he said, holding her arms. "I need to get another condom."

———

Flat on her back, legs sprawled wide, Regina thought about what they'd done and grinned. She hadn't expected to feel so happy about making love with Hunter, but she did. He was spectacular, everything she ever imagined he would be—and she'd imagined a lot over the years.

It was thoughtful of him to remember about protection, too, though she dared to admit to herself, at twenty-seven, she was ready to be a mother, ready for marriage.

Scowling, she wondered how Hunter felt about marriage. He hadn't shared much about his marriage while he was married, and not a thing about his divorce. She had no clue what had happened but figured sooner or later, he'd tell her. Though he likely wasn't too keen on the institution since he'd failed once, but then, you never know. It was too soon to think of that; they were just getting to know each other. Once the job was completed and they returned Matilda to her family, they could continue and grow their relationship.

She had no idea where he lived but since he worked in Chicago and she in the suburb of Groveland, just forty-five minutes away, they should be able to continue seeing each other.

She smiled as she thought of her mom and dad. They loved Hunter, back when they worked together. Her dad, being a retired cop, spent hours talking cop-shop with Hunter the times they saw each other, which wasn't often, though they got along great. Her mom would be happy if her youngest of three daughters finally married. Of her three older brothers and her two sisters, she was the only one not married. They would all be happy for her.

———

Fuck. It broke.

He saw it as soon as he'd pulled off the condom, then tossed it in the garbage can. Damn, it being so close to expiration, what could he expect?

He stood in front of the bathroom mirror, scowling at his reflection. Straightening up, he turned on the faucet, wet his hands and slicked them through his hair, pulling it off his forehead.

Should he tell her? He should tell her.

Damn, he knew she wanted to be in a relationship with him, and he with her, but having a baby was a completely different ball game. What were the chances she got pregnant this first time? After some thinking he decided it was a small chance, and if luck was on their side, she wouldn't be pregnant. Then he thought about her large Italian family. Two sisters and three brothers, all within a few years of each other. Shit.

He decided against telling her. No need to worry her needlessly. And a few months down the road, if he had knocked her up, he'd marry her. Hell, he'd marry her anyway if she wasn't pregnant.

Stalking into the guestroom he dumped the entire packet of condoms out and after carefully examining them, he found two that were damaged, two that weren't. He tossed the two that looked ripped in the wastebasket but kept the other two. Then he walked down the hall with the two in hand.

CHAPTER SIXTEEN

They drove from Groveland to Chicago, a forty-five-minute drive the next day and settled into a five-star hotel. Hunter's home was located nearly an hour north of Chicago, not convenient to the inner city where the house was located, hence the hotel reservation. Hunter paid for a suite with one bedroom only. She didn't protest—knew it would do no good, which was fine with her. She knew she loved Hunter and while they had the chance, she'd spend every minute she could with him.

Having passed the interview a few days ago, they'd been accepted into the 'house', and Hunter writing out the big check payment of $15,000 helped when he'd laid it down on the pastor's desk, before the interview began. The program in which they'd enrolled was for two weeks. She prayed they found Matilda quickly and safely got her out of there if they needed to in that time, if not earlier.

Regina gulped as she thought about the money. She'd grown up in modest, middle-class means and that kind of money was a windfall. Hunter treated it as though it was nothing.

Now, on the way to the 'house', Regina was sweating bullets, even though it wasn't all that warm outside this late September morning.

She could do this. She could. She'd trained to do this job, and she was ready. Still, she couldn't talk herself out of being nervous, especially since the pastor had explained, going into great detail about their initiation today. He'd been gleefully graphic about what she'd have to 'endure' and prove she wanted to be a submissive wife. Unfortunately, it was too late for second thoughts.

"What was the pastor's name again?" Regina asked.

"Robert Griffin," Hunter replied. "By the way, you look great in that dress," Hunter praised.

She gave him a puckish grin. "Pink isn't my color, but since you chose and paid for it, I'll wear it."

Smirking, he said, "You look like the perfect, submissive wife."

Reaching his hand over to her, he quickly flipped up her skirt so it landed almost to her groin and glanced down.

"Hunter!" she gasped, shoving her skirt down over her thighs.

"Do I have to stop the car and spank you?" he inquired softly.

He was one of those guys who, even when he was raging, didn't scare her, but when he talked softly it was another story. She shivered at his quiet tone.

"Do I?" he inquired.

She shook her head, knowing now—remembering why he'd tossed up her skirt.

"I want to see," he said. "No panties," he reminded her.

She cringed, slid her skirt up so he could easily see she wore none.

He looked away and nodded. "Good. Now, a bit of advice and a reminder. You need to react to my commands immediately. You must allow me to touch you whenever, wherever I want." He frowned. "Damn, we should have practiced longer."

"No. No. Sorry, you just caught me by surprise. I keep forgetting…"

"No-more-forgetting, got it?"

Regina's face burned at his words. Where was a drink when she needed one? She had suggested the two of them have a few before checking out of their hotel, but he said they didn't want to jeopardize getting into this house by showing up drunk, especially since the pastor told them no drugs or alcohol allowed in the place.

Looking down, she fingered the skirt of the dress, a sheer fabric over something smooth and shiny, set in waist, low scooped neck and long sleeves in pale pink. Never had she worn anything so feminine and short—mid thigh-length. Hell, it had been years since she'd worn a dress.

Gazing out the window she jumped, startled when a big, hard hand fell on her thigh. She stiffened until he reminded her.

"Uh-uh, relax."

She opened her mouth, ready to protest but calmed down when she remembered his words; that she had to allow him to touch her anytime, anyplace he wanted. Relaxing and slumping lower in her seat, she tried to pretend his touch didn't bother her. Then he started stroking her thigh, slipping beneath the hem of her dress, moving higher, squeezing it.

Her breath caught at his strong, yet sensitive touch and she shivered. She loved his hands on her—anywhere—but just thinking about going into this place and doing what they had to do left her feeling uneasy.

"Breathe," he ordered.

Regina's gasp sputtered out of her and she glared at him. "You just love taking advantage of me like this, don't you?"

"Remember those credit cards, darlin'," he purred.

She gave him a wide-eyed look. "I do. I'll even remind you about paying them once we're done with this job."

"Thanks," he snapped, removing his hand. "I still owe you, though, before I hand over the check. What happened after you left Chicago? Hadn't I set up your cards online for you with automatic monthly payments?"

"You did, but after a few months I had to sign into the accounts and lower the amount I could pay each month."

"And why is that?" he inquired.

"I had also bought my house and I had to get some new furniture and stuff," she muttered. "Are we almost there?" she asked, successfully changing the topic.

He chuckled. "Just like a little girl. A few more blocks and we're there. Calm down now, follow my lead, and we'll be done soon."

CHAPTER SEVENTEEN

Regina double-stepped to keep up with Hunter as he strode from the car to the double doors of the house. He wore a pinstriped charcoal colored suit, white shirt, powerhouse red tie. He looked yummy, she mused catching up with him.

He held the door open for her and as she stepped past him, he patted her ass and murmured, "Be a good girl now."

"I am always a good girl." She sniffed and swung her hips, then nearly stumbled in her heels.

He caught her around the waist. Lifting her chin, her nose in the air, she continued to walk slightly ahead of him—or he most likely chose to walk behind her, as he told her recently, for the 'view' was better.

"Better, much better," he purred.

They ended up in the pastor's office again, but it was empty. The two of them, side by side, as they held hands, walked down a corridor, following the sound of several voices.

They paused in front of double doors opened wide. Two men stood on either side of the doors, checked their ID's and allowed them inside.

Over her shoulder, Regina checked out the two men as she walked into the room. They sure as hell didn't look like church ushers to her, but out and out thugs. Regina narrowed her eyes on one of the men, knowing he was their plant as he immediately looked away and wouldn't meet her eyes, while the other man gave her a lewd smile.

Facing forward, she saw they'd entered a community room of sorts with several chairs positioned in a big circle, and one chair in the center. Damn. Memories returned then, flooding her brain, recalling what that one chair was for. Then her gaze zeroed in on the black leather paddle on the seat of the chair; it was big and round—big enough it would cover her whole ass. Damn…

Regina noted several people were already seated in the chairs, chatting amiably. Her gaze riveted then on the women in attendance and their manner of dress. They all wore short skirts, high heels (hers were lower heels as she hadn't managed how to walk in the stilts Hunter had purchased for her) and tight, revealing tops, or low necklines on their dresses. Obviously, as Hunter had chosen her clothing for this job, so had the men with their women, she assumed.

Frowning, she looked around suspiciously, even as Hunter led her to a vacant chair in the outer circle. She paused beside him as he sat down, noting there was only one chair. Not a problem she decided when he slid his arm around her waist and pressed her down to sit on one knee. Just then a man's friendly, boisterous voice broke through the chatting.

"Ah, our new members have arrived," Pastor Griffin said, from where he sat in the outer circle. The pastor was a baldheaded, big, gruff man, around sixty years old with a decided paunch. He wore a superior look which Regina immediately resented. "Everyone, welcome them."

Polite applause echoed in the community room and Regina felt her cheeks heat up. Damn, she hoped her face wasn't red. She smiled politely then glanced at Hunter who wore a friendly expression and hugged her closer to him.

"Introduce yourselves to our members," the pastor said.

Regina was tongue-tied—a good thing—since Hunter told her he'd do the talking.

"I'm Hunter Monroe," he said in his deep baritone, then smiled down at her. "And this is my lovely wife, Regina."

"Welcome," many voices intoned.

"All right," the pastor said, "we're all excited to have a new couple with us—it's been a few months—so let's get started with our meeting. First of all, would the Monroes please move to the chair in the center? We all know what happens now, don't we, friends?"

Regina noted the gleeful smirk on the pastor's face. Then she took a quick glimpse around the circle and saw most of the men wore the same expression, as did most of the women, with the exception of few. Regina focused on those two women, watched their expressions, noted how stiff they looked in their chairs. She wondered if one of them was their quarry, trying to recall what Matilda looked like in the picture Hunter had shown her.

Hunter rose from his chair and Regina had no choice but to stand from her position on his knee. Then he pulled her to the chair in the center of the circle. Regina's eyes widened as she watched him remove his suit jacket, drape it over the back of the chair, then roll his long sleeves up to his elbows. She gulped, her eyes riveted on his muscular arms, knowing what he was preparing for as she stood mutely beside him. He picked up the paddle, took his seat then and reached for her hand. Regina stood stiffly beside him, her face burning with heat. The pastor had warned them of this initiation and now that they were there she didn't know if she could go through with it.

As she stood there, her hands clasped tightly around her waist, she watched the pastor as he rose from his chair and walked to the center, joining them.

He looked around the circle at all of the couples nodding their heads. "This initiation is no surprise, of course, and everyone here has gone through it."

"Mrs. Monroe, over your husband's lap now and we'll begin," the pastor said then he returned to his seat. Meeting Hunter's eyes, seeing the stern, direct look on his face, made Regina shiver as he pulled on her hand, easily breaking her resistance, and eased her over his lap. Her toes touched the floor and her hair dragged over her face as she stared down at the tile floor, quivering. Damn, she'd faced guns before and never felt this vulnerable. She remained stiff as he raised her skirt up to the middle of her back, embarrassment flooding her as she thought of how everyone could see her bare ass.

"Hunter…" she began.

"Fuck," he said under his breath. "Keep still and silent." He looked up at Pastor Griffin once more. "How many did you say? I can't recall from our meeting or what's in the contract."

"Twenty-five, is the initiation number, right members?"

"Yes!" the mostly male voices shouted in unison.

Regina stiffened even as she focused on the floor.

"Relax," Hunter whispered. "This is why we practiced," he murmured, then laid the first slap on her ass.

Regina jolted, gasped, but managed to maintain her position. He'd gone easy with her with that one, then he delivered a second. They were barely love taps and she relaxed a bit more. She could get through this without making a scene if he maintained this little force.

After the fifth smack, the pastor interrupted. "Mr. Monroe," he said severely, "show your wife, who is here to become your submissive that you mean business."

What in the hell did he mean by that? she wondered.

"Just warming her up a bit," Hunter drawled.

She felt his hand tighten around her waist as he pulled her body tight against his, then he struck her again—much harder. She couldn't contain herself and shrieked in surprise.

"Better," the pastor said. "Continue."

Within moments Regina kicked her feet and squirmed as she tried to escape his hold. All he did was raise her a bit, adjusting her further up and over his lap then captured her legs together with one of his. When she couldn't budge, she collapsed over his knees, sniffled, cringing with each smack as she lost count. She wanted to cry but wouldn't allow herself to—this whole experience was humiliating, and she gathered her strength. She wouldn't let them see her cry!

Then heat sufficed both her face and her ass when the others all counted, shouting out the numbers until they reached twenty-five.

Suddenly, Hunter stopped. "Twenty-five," Hunter announced in a relieved tone, started helping her off his lap but stopped when the pastor spoke again.

"Keep her there, Mr. Monroe. You aren't through."

"That was the designated twenty-five," Hunter snapped.

Regina heard the fury in Hunter's voice, but he maintained his control.

"Your wife didn't cry."

"Was that a requirement?"

"An unspoken one," Pastor Griffin said. "Give her more until she does."

"No," Hunter snapped as he lifted Regina from his lap and rose with her.

"No?" the older man growled.

"No. She's had enough. This time."

The man bristled, straightened up, tugged down his vest before speaking. "Then I am afraid you are done here. No refunds, you know."

"Wait!"

Regina stood at Hunter's side, biting her lower lip. "We'll continue," she said.

Pastor Griffin looked at her, satisfied, then nodded. Regina turned to Hunter as he reluctantly returned to his seat. Looking at her with a questioning, angry expression.

Regina lowered herself over Hunter's knees again, prepared to put on an Oscar winning performance.

"Do it," she hissed when time lapsed, and he hadn't started again. "And make them count."

———

Hunter gritted his teeth together, raised his hand and slapped the paddle crisply on Regina's ass. Looking down, his face focused completely on her splotchy, pink skin. He kept up a brisk tempo, mesmerized as emotional pain filled him—as he knew it did her —only hers was physical pain.

He'd been with subs in the past who thoroughly enjoyed pain

—the harder the better for some—but this was new to Regina, and he knew she was no pain slut.

Her skin went from pink to red to purple and splotchy. Thank God she was shrieking, crying, sobbing and trying to escape him—the pastor would be pleased—when suddenly he stopped.

She'd been kicking her legs, her fingernails she'd dug into his calf until he stopped. That was twenty more he realized—enough.

He sat there with her draped across his lap, breathing heavily as he stared down at her. What in the hell? He'd been too rough —too hard on her. Her ass was a mottled purple with areas of red-no pink at all. He should simply end this—not continue with the job. Fuck!

"Excellent, Monroe. You made her cry. That was important. You may take Mrs. Monroe to the ladies room to freshen herself and return to the meeting. Bathroom is right down the hall and turn left."

Hunter met the pastor's 'holier than thou' expression as he carefully helped Regina to her feet. She trembled against him. He settled his arm around her waist as he guided her from the eerily silent room. He gave the thugs a cold look as he swept her past them, trying to understand the point of this initiation. He'd seen the way the one security guy looked at her and he didn't like it a bit. He glared at the man, then looked at the other who sported a passive expression. This was the infiltrator—good to know.

He stood outside the women's bathroom, arms folded as he leaned against the wall, waiting for Regina to come out.

Soon she exited the bathroom, walking carefully and rubbing her butt.

"Damn, we should have left," he snarled as he slid his arm around her waist. Reaching down he carefully patted her backside, but she moved out of his embrace.

"Hurts," she simply said and took his arm, walked beside him. "I don't know if I can go back inside right now," she said softly, biting her lip again, looking down at the floor.

"Requirement," he said. "Should be over soon."

Inside, they returned to Hunter's seat. He settled Regina

down carefully on his knee, but she popped up as soon as she sat down and stood beside him, instead, color flagging her cheeks. He saw her face was filled with utter humiliation and fury tore through him as he decided wringing the pastor's neck was a strong possibility.

"Why, Mrs. Monroe, this meeting goes another hour. Please, take a seat," Pastor Griffin said.

"I can't," she snapped, and she stood behind Hunter's chair, holding onto it.

"You will be a distraction standing, so I advise you to sit down. Take heart, next meeting you will have your own chair, same as the others."

Hunter took her hand and pulled her to sit gingerly on his lap again.

"Excellent," the pastor said, and resumed the meeting.

Regina sat with her arm around Hunter's shoulder, her legs positioned between his. He held her there, at one point jumped when he felt moisture hit his hand. Quickly glancing up he saw tears falling from Regina's eyes. He stifled his groan and kept his hand around her waist, holding her against him.

Damn. He guessed it was a combination of pain and humiliation that caused her tears as he held her carefully.

After listening to the shithead pastor go on and on about women submitting to their husbands and/or boyfriends and the joy it would bring them, fury had set in. If the meeting didn't end in five, he was out of there. It ended shortly and he stood up, picked Regina up in his arms and walked from the community room, their room key in hand.

He ignored all of the members' friendly overtures to them as he strode out of the room. She hadn't said a word—not a fucking word but laid her head on his shoulder. This worried him. They reached their room and he put her down on her feet as he shoved the key into the slot and opened the door.

Once inside, he slammed the door shut and locked it, emptied his pockets of his change and keys—his phone had been left behind at home as they weren't allowed. He'd also left his and Regina's guns in the car—no need for that at a church the contract said. But Hunter saw bulges in the suit jackets of security outside the community room—holsters he guessed—with guns.

Someone had carried in their luggage and Regina lugged hers onto the bed, unlocked and opened it, dug around inside.

For the first time since they left the community room, she looked up at him, met his gaze. He saw the redness in her eyes and groaned. Shoving a hank of hair back from his forehead he moved carefully to where she stood, took her in his arms and held her against his chest for a moment, then released her.

"You went beyond the call of duty, sweetheart. Sorry," he whispered.

Still not meeting his eyes, she riffled through her clothes. "Won the academy award, didn't I?"

He tilted her chin up. "Look at me." She shook her head and he added roughly, "I said look-at-me."

Slowly her head came up and she looked into his eyes. He saw the pain in them, humiliation, and something else but didn't know what.

He leaned down, nuzzled her neck as he wound his arms around her. "Remember, cameras," he whispered.

Hunter felt her stiffen in his arms, but sighed, relieved when she wound her arms around his waist.

"Thanks for the reminder."

While she'd been rummaging around in her luggage, he'd been glancing around the room, noting the tiniest equipment he'd ever seen. Most people wouldn't even notice the small devices.

He dipped his head and proceeded to kiss her—and kiss her —leaving her breathless. Lifting his head, he asked, loud enough for a camera to pick up. "How about I rub some pain ointment on you?"

She gave him a quizzical look, but sudden understanding filled her face.

"Yes, but I want to get changed into something else."

He stepped back with a nod. "No panties, though," he reminded her. "Change in the bathroom," he murmured.

She moved to her suitcase, snatched up a short skirt and silky white blouse and made her way to the bathroom.

Within moments she returned wearing only the white blouse.

He pointed from where he sat on the side of the bed. "On your stomach, in the middle."

She nodded and obliged him.

"Raise your arms up over your head," he advised.

She was reluctant at first and he guessed it was because she knew her ass would be on display for the cameras, but they had no choice. Regina raised them above her head, clasped them together on the mattress.

Stifling a groan at the sight of her mottled, purple-red skin he squeezed ointment on his hands, rubbed them together then carefully touched her. She sobbed but quickly stopped when he continued massaging the cream into her cheeks. His heart raced as he looked down at her, felt his cock tighten, throb. Damn! He was aroused at the sight of her like this, but ashamed he'd caused her pain and discomfort. He was a dominant, but no sadist as he'd told her.

His idea of dominance was obedience from his submissive, some pain for pleasure, but nothing like this. To his mind this was abuse, though for some subs he'd seen at the clubs, they wouldn't think so. Some of them were definitely pain sluts, but not Regina he knew.

CHAPTER EIGHTEEN

Regina couldn't help the groan that escaped her as Hunter's hands rubbed in the cream over her sore cheeks. It felt good but hurt—a lot—but truly he'd had no choice. She knew that in her heart he wasn't into dealing out this level of pain, but there was nothing they could do, with all of the eyes of the members and pastor on them.

This paddling was worse than any by ten times at the minimum of what he'd given her in the past. She hated it, but not him.

And when the pastor said they'd have to leave she was furious; they needed to find Matilda fast. Earlier, as they'd walked past the members, her gaze flitted over the women, until she paused on a woman who resembled the picture she'd seen of Matilda, but instead of brown hair, hers was blonde. This woman appeared sad and scared, and not happy to be there. Regina's eyes then flitted to the man next to her, seemingly holding her hand—too tightly —keeping her beside him. He wore that lewd expression she'd seen on the pastor's face, his eyes on Regina as he leaned over and whispered in the young woman's ear.

Matilda closed her eyes and nodded slightly at whatever he said and, if Regina wasn't mistaken, she thought she saw the young woman lean a bit away from him as tears filled her eyes.

"Done," Hunter said as he closed the cover on the tube and laid it down on the bedside table.

She sat up, gingerly, and pulled on her skirt. "Come in the bathroom with me," she said so softly he almost missed her request.

He raised his brow as she moved carefully from the bed and followed her into the bathroom. He shut the door behind them and glanced around, trying not to be obvious as he looked for more cameras. Ah, above the shower curtain in a corner was one.

He glanced down when he felt her loop her arms around his neck, nuzzling him there with her lips.

"Hey, hey, baby," he whispered, silently questioning her motives, winding his arms around her waist, pulling her flush against him.

"I saw her," she murmured, enjoying having an excuse to be in his arms.

"Did you?"

As she continued kissing his neck, she said, "Yes. She did not look happy. She looked scared. Why don't you take a walk around and see if you can find what room she's in?"

"I planned on it later, after dark, when I know everyone will be in their rooms."

She nodded. "Good."

Swiping his hand down her back, he added, "Thought I'd pretend I was lost and enter the wrong room."

"Hmm, think you need a better idea," she said, "what, I've no idea though." She sighed then stepped back, releasing him.

Regina opened the door and moved into the bedroom suite. There was a sofa, coffee table and TV so she sank down carefully on the sofa with a grimace, smoothed her skirt and leaned to one side, putting her weight on her hip. She grabbed the remote and flicked on the news—loud.

"Uh, think you can turn that down a tad?" Hunter asked as he blocked the TV.

She gave him a meaningful look. "We need to talk." *Hint, hint.*

Hunter sank down beside her in understanding, then leaned close to her ear as he slid one hand between her thighs.

Regina jumped, startled at his touch. She'd forgotten she was sans panties. "What are you doing?" she asked loud enough he could hear, knowing their host wouldn't hear her though due to the television's volume.

"You need an orgasm," he said.

Hearing laughter in his voice she smiled, the first authentic smile she'd given him since they arrived.

"I think you're right, but how is that going to help us figure out the location of you know who?"

"It won't but it'll relax you—besides, as I said, you need one."

Sitting forward, turning sideways, he spread her legs apart, raised her skirt to her lap then sank to his knees between them, leaning toward her sweet spot. She gasped when he flicked his tongue along her labia, licking the folds until he reached her clit, where he flicked her harder with a flat tongue.

"Hunter," she groaned, "Please…"

"What I'm aiming for," he grunted as he continued a full out assault on her clitoris until she shrieked then groaned her pleasure. She sank down, started to close her legs since he'd moved back but he kept her legs open. "Nope. Another one."

"No!" Regina exclaimed. "You're driving me nuts!"

"That's the plan, only this time it'll be different."

And it was different—more intense, leaving her delirious, hot and on edge, not relaxed as she usually would be after having one —but wanting to have another, of which he obliged her moments later. And one more…

Regina couldn't believe he'd eaten her, given her three orgasms in a row when she was lucky to get one in an evening with a guy—though there hadn't been many guys she admitted— nor had she had all that many orgasms.

"Stop, please," she begged.

He scooped her up in his arms as he walked her to the bed, laid her down gently and ordered, "Take a nap. I'll wake you in a couple hours as we're having an early supper with the group. I'll be back in a bit."

She watched him leave the suite and close the door behind him. She scrambled from the bed, tried to open the door but the handle wouldn't budge. Damn! He'd locked her in? She fumed as she stalked back to the bed. What in the hell? Why would he lock her in…unless he meant to do something dangerous? But the plan was for her to back-up so that didn't make sense. She wished she had her Glock 43 with her but Hunter said no guns allowed inside the church. She felt naked without it, especially in this situation.

She rose from the bed, tried the door once more. Damn, locked solid. And the pastor had given only him a key. Shit. She opened the curtains and saw their suite overlooked the parking lot. Sweeping the lot, she saw Hunter sauntering down the row of vehicles, hands in his pockets, seemingly taking a walk on a fine autumn day, but she knew what he was doing—checking out license plates and likely memorizing more than a few at a time. He had a remarkable memory.

Once he returned, he'd use his computer to email what he'd found to a cop-friend of theirs at the station.

———

Supper that evening in the main dining room was enjoyable, Hunter thought, surprised. There were nine couples present, which made for lively conversation.

He'd found out which vehicle belonged to Matilda's boyfriend and planned on getting into it sooner than later to check it out. He'd learned from the informant, who'd happened to follow him outside when he'd gone for his walk, that Matilda and her boyfriend had been there already for several weeks. The minimum one could pay was for the two weeks Hunter paid, but a couple could stay there for months—as long as they kept paying.

Regina sat on his left side, speaking softly with a woman on her right. Unfortunately, it wasn't Matilda, but another woman who'd been at the house for over a month, with her new husband.

He cringed when he heard her praising the church and pastor and her learning what to do to make hers and her husband's marriage happier. She'd laughed when Regina softly inquired if she enjoyed the somewhat rough treatment.

"Do I love it?" she said. "Some of it, yes, some no, but Adam loves it all."

"So you simply tolerate it then and believe it will help your marriage?" Regina asked.

The young woman, whose name Hunter learned was Mary Jane, simply nodded. Then he caught her whispered, "And Adam's a real tiger in bed once he's disciplined me."

Hunter sighed and thought so Mary Jane was one of the pain sluts, he mused, or rather she put up with it for the end result of hot sex with her husband.

"I'll be sorry when we leave next week. It's been a wonderful experience," Mary Jane added, "but we have run out of money."

Her tinkling laughter made Regina cringe.

Regina simply nodded, gave the woman and smile then turned to Hunter and raised her brows.

Smiling, Hunter could imagine what Regina's thoughts were. *What in the hell? Is this woman nuts or what?*

Across the table and down to the left sat Matilda with her boyfriend. She did not look happy—not at all. Hunter saw the redness in her eyes and assumed she'd been crying.

"I'm going to approach Matilda once we're done eating," Regina murmured.

Hunter shook his head. "No." When she opened her mouth likely to protest, he added, "Too soon. We need to be here at least a few days before we do something like that."

She muttered, "If I survive."

The meal ended and all Hunter wanted to do was crash for the night.

The pastor rose to his feet at the head of the table with his wine glass raised. "Once again, we'd like to welcome the Monroe couple, who will be staying with us for two weeks."

"Here, here," the men said, and everyone took a sip of their wine.

"And now we've come to an important part of our day. It's maintenance spanking time, ladies!" he announced with glee.

Then he looked directly at Regina. "Call it a nightly bedtime ritual."

"What in the hell?" Hunter said under his breath, tightening his fingers around his wine glass.

"What is that? Maintenance spanking?" Regina asked loud enough everyone heard her.

He heard the laughs from the men at the table and saw the women cringe.

Hunter had never talked to her about that, never thought of it and the pastor hadn't mentioned it. Maybe this would only apply to the others there, and not them as newbies. And he'd read the contract and didn't see that item specifically delineated.

He watched Regina's face pale as she watched every single man at the table rise, grab his woman's hand, and leave the dining room. Only the two of them sat there, until the pastor, who was the last to leave, turned to them.

"Come along. You will be participating also," he said. "Into the library this time, though, not the community room."

"I don't recall seeing this in the contract," Hunter said.

"Oh, well, it's only for fun—something we established a long time ago—but it is necessary for all to participate—no exceptions," he stated firmly.

Hunter rose from his chair, scowling, and assisted Regina to her feet. As they followed the pastor out, Regina whispered, "I can't take any more punishment today, Hunter. I can't!"

"He said it's more for fun and not punishment. I promise to go easy on you."

"Right," she said dryly. "So explain what this is—this mainte-nance thingie."

"It's a term used by couples that practice domestic discipline in a relationship. The head of household sets up a maintenance spanking for whatever days of a week to spank his sub, reminding her to be good. It could simply be one day a week, or every day, intensity to be determined by the HOH."

"HOH?" Regina asked as she walked along with him.

"Head of Household."

"So that's what you are considered to be in our relationship? Sort of same as a Dom then?"

He nodded with a frown. "Did you read any of the contract?"

She nodded. "A bit. So, okay. This is probably more like spanking for fun and titillation then?"

Hunter said, "Purely up to the HOH."

"Uh-huh. So you've done this before?"

"No. I've never been in a long-term relationship with a sub."

They arrived at the library, which was massive, and Hunter watched Regina's face. Shocked, stunned, mouth agape, her eyes widened on the display before them.

———

"Oh, my God," Regina whispered.

"Breathe deep, baby. Take it easy," Hunter instructed as he pulled her inside.

Regina couldn't believe her eyes. There was a long leather-clad bench that ran the length of an entire wall, positioned in front of floor to ceiling windows overlooking a garden. Directly in front of the bench and attached to the wall on either end was a ballet barre type railing. Over that bench the women had draped themselves, hands clutching the railings. They'd raised their skirts to their waists (or maybe the HOH's had) and their asses were all naked—every one of them.

"Come, Mrs. Monroe, the ladies have saved a spot for you."

Regina gulped. "Uh, well, I don't believe I'm participating in this event," she said, even as Hunter took her arm and propelled her over to the bench. She looked up anxiously at him.

"You have to. I said I'd go easy on you," he whispered.

There was a place at the very end of the row for Regina. With a strong arm he pressed her stiff body over the railing, kicked her feet apart a bit and tossed her skirt up over her back, revealing her naked ass as well.

Regina cringed, held onto the railing.

Hunter not only owed her for doing the job, but for pain and humiliation beyond anything she'd ever felt before.

Suddenly, dramatic music started up in the room, and the pastor shouted, "Ready, everyone!"

Regina looked behind her, along the long line of men standing behind and to one side of their women, their choice of disciplinary tool in hand. Paddles, both leather and wood, some large, some small, a riding crop or two, a cane, all had an instrument except for Hunter, who stood there with his hand raised near her back side.

"Begin!" the pastor shouted, even as explosions of strikes echoed through the room, followed by women groaning, moaning and some shrieking, and some stomping feet.

"Breathe deep, Regina. It should help a bit," Hunter ordered as he slammed his hand against her lower buttocks, where her thighs met her ass.

Her breath exploded from her even as she screamed and reached back to cover her ass. "Damn you," she growled. "You said a light hand."

"I'm only using my hand," he said softly. "And I'm hitting territory that's a bit more virgin. Only ten," he said. "Nine more…"

He caught up with the men as apparently, this crazy disciplinary session was supposed to be done in time together to the music.

Cringing and keeping her eyes shut, Regina escaped to her own little world of pain as Hunter continued.

CHAPTER NINETEEN

The last slap delivered, Hunter helped Regina from the bar, and her skirt fell down, covering what he knew was her sore ass. The other couples left the library, women rubbing their asses as well, scowling, and men striding alongside them with big grins on their faces. Hunter knew that feeling—had experienced it himself, and it was fine if agreeable to everyone involved. But he couldn't help but notice a few of the women with tears flowing from their angry eyes, glaring at their mates. So much for being fun, he mused dryly.

"Wait just a minute, Mr. Monroe."

Hunter looked over at the pastor heading their way.

"I distinctly heard the Mrs. swear at you. She deserves another ten for that, according to the contract you signed."

Hunter's lips tightened even as Regina asked, "Is that true?"

The pastor glared at her. "Didn't you read what you signed?"

"She did," Hunter inserted quickly. He nodded over to the bench. "Get back in place."

Regina glared at both men as they waited.

"Unless you're ready to leave…" the pastor said.

"No. I'm going," she muttered, even as she bent over the padded bench and grabbed the railing.

"You either want to make your husband happy in this relationship, or you don't, Mrs. Monroe. Purely your choice. I will leave the two of you but know there are devices in place, noting your activity," he warned. He started to leave then paused, went over to a table and picked up a heavy, rectangular shaped wooden paddle drilled with several holes. "Use this, Mr. Monroe. She won't give you any problems after a session with it."

Hunter growled in protest, but Regina intervened.

"Get on with it, husband," she whispered.

"Regina..." he began but she stopped him.

"Just do it. I need to learn to keep my big mouth shut."

The pastor nodded in satisfaction, then left.

Hunter lifted her skirt once more and she grasped the railing tight as he quickly delivered ten swats with the heavy paddle, and all she could do was sob. He'd tried to keep them light, but the design of the paddle made it impossible, no matter what strength one used, for the victim to feel every swat. Hard. He finished, threw down the paddle and eased her to her feet.

"I don't think I can walk," she whispered.

Her sobbing intensified when he lifted her into his arms and walked her out of the library and down the hall to their suite. Hunter set her down on her feet, went to the dresser and dug out one of his t-shirts. He undressed her then put her in the t-shirt, pantiless, then laid her down on the bed, on her stomach. He sat beside her.

"Sleep, try and sleep," he whispered.

And she did.

———

During the middle of the night, Regina wakened in utter pain, and not just her ass, but agony filled her entire body, head to toe.

As she raised up onto her forearms there was a bit of light coming into the room from the bathroom night light. Then she felt a body beside her. Hunter. He appeared to be sound asleep and she rolled over, away from him, ready to hit the bathroom and find some Ibuprofen when Hunter spoke.

"Meds on the table next to you," he murmured.

She sat up as carefully as she could, but it didn't prevent the squeak of protest from her. He reached over and stroked her back.

"Sorry, sweetheart," he said.

Regina didn't say a word but gulped down the water and pills, came to her feet and started to work her way to the bathroom. Hunter was immediately at her side.

"I'll carry you," he said.

She pushed him back with a hand. "I can do this. I'm fine," she murmured.

Hunter stepped back but she saw the scowl on his face. Let him scowl, though she couldn't see he had anything to be pissed about.

Heaving a sigh, she slowly made her way to the bathroom and closed the door behind her. She gingerly sat down on the toilet and gasped even as tears leaked from her eyes. Hurt—pain—unlike anything she'd ever felt in her life encompassed her. She had to get out of this hell hole—had to—preferably with Hunter's client in tow. She could just imagine the poor woman being forced to stay there, forced to accept this unbearably painful abuse from her boyfriend, against her will, for as long as the bastard kept her there.

For the first time, Regina realized Hunter had actually gone light on her at home during their training sessions, but under the pastor's watchful eye, this wasn't the case. Damn the wretched man. She'd love nothing better than to smash the pastor's ass over that bench in the library with the paddle Hunter had used on her, then cut off his balls afterwards.

There was a difference between pain for pleasure and pain for hurting someone, and the man obviously expected women to be hurt.

A small knock sounded on the door, followed by Hunter's voice.

"You okay, Regina?"

She gulped after taking care of business, rose to her feet and tugged down the t-shirt he'd dressed her in. She opened the door and met his worried expression. Looking over her shoulder, reminded of the location of the camera, she put her arms around his waist and laid her head down on his chest. She whispered, "I'll live, but I don't know how much more of this I can take."

"One more day," he promised, "then we'll get to Matilda and find out the truth of the matter."

Hunter returned her to bed, and they slept hard until sun filtered in through the sides of the curtains on the windows.

———

Breakfast that next morning was uneventful; no more public humiliation, Hunter mused, until the pastor rose from his place at the end of the table.

"All of you each have your classes, based on where you are in the program, so you may all leave, with the exception of the Monroes."

Hunter caught Regina's surprised expression, saw her gulp down the lump in her throat as the others left them alone with the pastor.

He looked between the two of them. "So, we are on day two, and here is your schedule." The pastor handed over a printed document to Hunter, who skimmed it, frowning.

"Since I don't recall this in the original contract as part of the training," Hunter said, "I'd like to see our signed copy first."

"That's fine. Come to my office then show up by one at the parlor."

The pompous man left the dining room and Regina questioned Hunter. "What gives? What don't you remember reading?" She reached for the document, but he kept it out of her reach.

"Hunter," she growled.

He growled back. "Regina. Remember your place and your attitude, or do you require an adjustment now, before we return to our suite?"

"Sorry, sir," she said, catching on quickly from the look Hunter gave her and his angry words.

"We'll read this in our suite, and this time, dear wife, you will read it in its entirety."

In their suite they sank down on the sofa, side by side, and once Hunter read the first page, he passed it to Regina. All four pages were passed, and Regina groaned when she finished and sank her head against the back of the sofa.

Hunter whispered, "You can always have it covered over later."

Regina snapped, "What difference will it make? I don't plan on showing my ass off to anyone else, so it may as well be your name tattooed on it."

Hunter couldn't believe some of the rules he'd admittedly skimmed over himself, including this one, which was happening today. He was to take Regina to a tattoo parlor in the church basement, and have his name tattooed on her ass, within a heart, the size to encompass nearly one-half of one entire cheek. To say he was stunned was putting it mildly, yet something inside him made him realize he wasn't totally against the idea. He'd already made his decision he wanted Regina in his life—permanently— and this provided his mark on her. But what stopped him was this would, once again, involve pain to Regina.

He sighed and whispered, "Anything else stand out in that contract to you?"

"Yes," she griped. "You are to not only spank me when I swear but wash my mouth out with soap? Good, God, Hunter, that is archaic, and no way can I see how all of this would ever help a couple have a good marriage."

"I know." He sighed, his eyes meeting hers. "You're tough. You can deal with this. I owe you, big time, Regina."

He came to his feet. "I'll be right back."

She sighed, knowing not to ask him where he was going but said, "Please, don't lock the door. It's not necessary."

He glared at her over his shoulder, his hand on the doorknob. "Don't leave. I'll be back by 11:30 for lunch in the dining room, followed by our visit to the tattoo parlor."

She groaned. "Can't we skip those two events? I'm just not in the mood for—"

A flashing light in the corner of the living area caught Hunter's eye and he knew how surveillance equipment worked. They were being watched and recorded right now.

"Be ready, or suffer the consequences," he warned harshly. His eyes darted to the corner once more and Regina caught the movement—the warning from him.

"Yes, sir, I will," she said, obedience in her tone.

She watched him close the door and she started chewing her lip. Earlier, she'd smelled chlorine in the building and guessed they had a pool. Hmm…

———

Regina settled into the water on the shallow end of an infinity pool with built in benches. It was amazing, Regina decided as she floated on her back. She wore a hot pink polka-dotted bikini Hunter had chosen that barely covered her. Still, it was quiet, pleasant here, until the silence was broken by voices.

She dropped her feet from her floating position and treaded water, her eyes on two women entering the pool room. The women dropped their towels and cover-ups on chairs then made their way down the pool steps; one woman started swimming laps while the other woman hovered on the steps, her gaze on Regina, but said nothing.

"Water's nice and warm," Regina said casually as she neared the woman. The woman was Matilda, and she seemed hesitant to speak to Regina as she hugged the side and sat on the steps.

Reaching her side, Regina whispered, "I know there are cameras, but do you know if they pick up our voices?"

She shook her head.

Regina said, "No to audio then."

The woman nodded.

Breathing a relieved sigh, Regina said, "Then we need to be quick, Matilda."

The young woman nodded slowly.

"Nod or shake your head at my questions."

Matilda's gaze darted around the pool area and she gasped just as her boyfriend entered the pool room.

Damn! "Are you being kept here against your will?"

Matilda's eyes widened as she gave Regina a pleading look, as her boyfriend headed toward them—quickly—Regina noticed.

Matilda nodded and Regina closed her eyes and relaxed, floating away as the boyfriend stopped beside Matilda.

Satisfaction soared through Regina that she'd asked the one most important question—and got her answer.

Matilda's boyfriend roared in anger at Matilda. The other woman swimming the short laps quickly left the pool, grabbed her towel and ran out.

Regina couldn't figure out why the rush when Matilda's boyfriend roughly snatched her out of the pool. Then he slung her over his right shoulder and made his way to the chair, his big palm striking her ass the entire time, scolding her.

"You know you're not supposed to go anywhere here at the house without me. Sneaking out is not allowed, Matilda."

He had to be a foot taller than the poor young woman and he reached the chair, snatched up her towel and cover-up and tossed them over the other shoulder. He paused as he reached the doorway out of the pool room, yanked down her bikini bottoms and started whaling on her ass again as he left the room, poor Matilda kicking, flailing, and shrieking in protest.

Regina glared after them then gulped when Hunter suddenly appeared in his black, tight, swim trunks. Damn, the man, he looked good.

He dove into the pool on the deep end then quickly and proficiently made his way to her side.

Pausing next to her they faced each other, treading water when she whispered, "You saw."

"Yeah, I got a gander at her ass which appeared swollen and redder than yours was last night," he growled. "Turns out the women can't be here in the pool room, or anywhere else in the building alone. One of the thugs came knocking on my door and told me to get down here and keep an eye on you."

"No audio," she murmured, barely opening her mouth to speak.

"Well, I wouldn't put it past the pastor and his thugs to be able to read lips."

Hunter located the devices in two corners then turned her so her back was to both of them. Then he started kissing her.

"What are you doing?" she whispered, her arms winding around his shoulders.

"Diversion in case we're being watched."

"That was Matilda. She's here against her will."

Hunter's eyes widened as he released her. "Now how in the hell do you know it's her?"

"Seen her picture enough. It's her, only much skinnier and haggard looking. She never opened her mouth. I told her to nod or shake her head when I asked her a question and she did. I got in that one question before the Neanderthal showed up and she nodded yes."

"So her parents were right then. We move tomorrow to get her out. We'll work out a plan tonight. It's nearly lunch time so we need to leave. We don't want to cause any suspicion at this point."

She nodded. "Right." Side by side they swam to the step. As they dried off with the towels they'd brought along and dropped at the pool's side, she saw him scowling.

"Now what?" she asked, exasperated.

He jammed his hands on his hips. "You know I have to discipline you and they need to know that—see it."

"Why?"

"Cause the rules are wherever you go in the place I need to accompany you. You came down here without me."

"I had no idea!" she protested.

He sighed. "It's in the contract which you didn't read."

"Hunter, no!" she shouted, even as he grabbed her arm and dragged her over to a lounge chair, sank down on it and yanked her over his lap.

"They'll expect this," he whispered.

Hunter's jaw tightened and he grimaced as he yanked down her bottoms and started slapping her ass.

Kicking and screaming did no good, Regina soon learned. After he'd slapped her at least twenty times he shoved her off his lap, yanked up her suit bottom, stood up and grabbed her arm, dragging her out of the pool room.

In their suite Regina ran to the bathroom and slammed the door, humiliated once again. Looking at her face in the mirror she saw she'd turned red. Turning around she pulled down her bottoms and saw the purpling of her ass had gotten even darker.

Through the closed door, she heard Hunter. "Come on, we don't have time to use anything on you right now."

"I'm just washing my face, damn it," she snapped.

When she opened the door, he sighed. "Damn, I have to do it again."

"No!" Regina wailed and started to run to the door.

He easily caught her and held her against him. "Stop it," he warned then dragged her over to the bed and tossed her over the foot of it. Holding her down with a hand at the back of her neck, he raised his hand with a sigh, knowing he had to keep up the act.

CHAPTER TWENTY

Lunch, thankfully, was uneventful and now Hunter had hold of Regina's elbow as he escorted her to the tattoo parlor located in the house's basement.

He'd forced himself earlier to smack her five times.

Regina wouldn't look at him or speak to him. He sighed, deciding he couldn't blame her. They had to get out of this place ASAP.

As they entered the room Hunter immediately looked around and couldn't find any security cameras.

A guy big as a linebacker, and tattooed heavily, strolled out from a back room and stopped behind a long counter.

"Hunter and Regina Monroe," Hunter said.

The guy sat down behind a computer, found their names and looked up at Hunter. "The usual, I imagine?"

"Can you show us a picture of the usual?" Regina asked.

The guy raised his brow then looked at Hunter.

"Yes, show us some shots of the usual."

The big guy wore a name tag with 'Tank' on it. Flickering his gaze over the brawny man, Hunter decided the name suited him.

Digging beneath his counter Tank pulled out a huge loose-leaf binder with photographs enclosed in plastic sleeves. "Take a look, but I'll tell you now, it's like looking at the same photo over and over again."

Hunter wondered at his annoyed response but opened the first page, then continued paging through it with Regina looking down at the book as she stood beside him.

"So basically our choices are a big heart encompassing one ass cheek with a name in the middle. That's it?"

"Yep, but a few couples have gotten a bit more innovative and the pastor didn't complain."

Thinking about the contract, which Hunter had read thoroughly, it said Regina would need to bear the tattoo with his name in the middle, but it didn't specify size.

"We'll have the same but, no larger than one inch square for heart size."

"Hey, man, it'll be tough getting your name in the middle of a tattoo that size," Tank said.

"But can it be done? My bride has never had a tattoo and I don't think she can tolerate the pain of it, unless you do it real small."

"Sure," he said, "but you do know the ass is the most sensitive area to tattoo. Right?"

"I don't give a shit what the pastor wants. How about the hip?" Hunter asked.

"Not near as painful, but the pastor always insists on the ass."

"Tough. She's my wife, not the pastor's. The hip, left side," he said.

"Hunter?" Regina began, "Do we want to take a chance on inciting the pastor's anger?"

"If he wants his damned money. He's lucky we're participating at all in this stupid-ass shit."

Tank led them into a back room and Hunter paused as he saw a reclining chair and a table.

"Chair or table?" Tank asked.

"I think the table."

"Oh, I'll be fine in the chair. It reclines and looks real comfy," Regina stated.

Hunter nodded. "We'll try it."

"Get undressed, Mrs. Monroe," Tank said.

"Completely?" Regina said with a gasp.

Tank pointed to a curtained room. "There are robes in there. Just put on one of the short ones."

"But I'm not having my butt tattooed," she protested.

"The hip is to the side so yep, same general area. No worries, ma'am, if you're modest. I can cover your lower area with a towel I can move around as needed."

Within a few moments, Regina came out, tying the belt on the robe. Hunter guided her down into the chair which reclined, and she lay on her side. Within minutes he knew the chair wouldn't work.

Regina screamed at the first touch of the needle and jerked away from Tank. "What the fuck?" she gasped.

"Hold still, damn it," Tank growled.

She stilled but with the next stab she shot up again. "Forget it," she said. "That hurts too much!"

She scrambled out of the chair and Tank sighed as she headed to the dressing room. "No way," she added.

Hunter grabbed her before she went inside, hauled her up into his arms and laid her down on the table. Before she could think about moving away again Tank produced a pair of cushioned handcuffs and Hunter restrained her wrists to the undersides of the table, then quickly brought up a restraint that went over her waist to prevent her from squirming.

Kicking her legs, Regina shouted, "Forget it, Hunter! I don't want a tattoo. I never wanted one," she protested.

Ignoring her he cuffed her ankles as well to the table and Tank proceeded with his work.

She screamed when Tank continued where he left off. After a few minutes she settled down, even though tears cascaded down her face.

"Almost done, sweetheart," Hunter said as he stood and watched Tank move with remarkable speed to tattoo the heart on her hip.

Then Tank turned off the motor and rose from his rolling stool.

"Damn, woman, you have no pain tolerance. How in the hell are you surviving in this place?" he muttered as he smeared petroleum jelly over the small heart and covered it with a square band aid.

"As you can see, not too well," Hunter said dryly.

He didn't release her immediately as he wanted her to calm down some first.

"Take off the damned cuffs," she eventually snarled.

"Hang tight a sec, Regina." Awkwardly, Hunter patted her shoulder and whispered in her ear, "You don't know how glad I am there are no cameras in this room because I sure as hell don't want to have to punish you again, especially after surviving this."

That seemed to quiet her down a bit and soon he released her from her bonds.

She shot up from the table, scrambled into the changing room and was out in minutes. She tore out of the room and Hunter barely made the same elevator to take them up to the main floor.

He jammed his finger at the stop button and the elevator came to a jarring halt. Hunter turned to Regina who had sank against the back wall, pouting, tears still in her eyes.

Caging her against the wall, his hands on either side of her head, he leaned forward and kissed her forehead. "You don't know how sorry I am for the pain this caused you, Regina. Know that tomorrow we'll be out of this shithole. Okay?"

She sniffed with her arms folded across her chest as she glared at him, teary-eyed. "Promise?" she whispered.

"Promise," he stated firmly.

She pulled herself forward and launched into Hunter's arms. After another cry or two she leaned back and looked down at his waistline.

"How in the hell did you survive getting your tattoo?"

"A bottle of tequila and plenty of encouragement from a couple other cops," he said with a laugh.

That evening, Hunter convinced the pastor that Regina was ill with the flu and wouldn't be down to dinner or be participating in the after dinner 'games'. He brought a tray of food up for himself, and in the bathroom, where Regina lolled in the bathtub, shared it with Regina.

The two of them spent the evening in their room, relaxing, and watching TV, speaking little due to the cameras and audio in the room—but they managed to come up with a plan to remove Matilda from the house.

———

The next day was a free day for the couples to do as they wished. Hunter would love nothing better than to spend the day in bed with Regina but knew they couldn't afford to waste any time.

The plan was he would distract Connor Johnson, Matilda's boyfriend, while Regina snuck Matilda from the house. It was a simple plan and Hunter hoped it would work. But not only would he have to distract Connor but the guards at the house as well. And what was the best way to plan a distraction? A fight, of course.

Hunter happened to know that at ten each morning, Connor worked out in the gym and he headed that way, knowing Regina would soon likely be headed for Matilda's suite.

Inside the gym Hunter scoped out the place, saw several other men working out, then zoned in on Connor who had donned a pair of boxing gloves and was attacking a bag.

Casually, Hunter yanked on a pair of gloves, then headed toward Connor, pausing beside him.

"You up for a round?" he asked.

Connor—build tall and lean—leaner than Hunter even, looked like he might be able to handle himself. But Hunter had been fooled by guys before.

Connor grinned, teeth big and white.

"Sure, old man," he drawled, turned and headed to the opposite side of the gym to the ring.

Hunter followed, swearing under his breath. Old man, my ass, he mused, thinking he couldn't wait to fuck this guy up good.

They climbed over the ropes and into the ring on opposite ends then started dancing toward each other. Within minutes they'd attracted a crowd and they chose sides, betting on the side Hunter noticed. Getting into position he noticed the two guards also entered the gym. Good. Regina would now have the opportunity to get Matilda out of this shithole.

Around round three Hunter was still standing, still strong but absorbed a surprise jab to the left side of his face and went down. Damn, he mused, that little shit. Thought he was a wise ass, did he? Sure, Hunter knew he was likely ten years older, still, generally, nothing distracted him—but something did. Five men in a group were tossing money at one guy. Hunter thought it was betting but he was stunned to see small cellophane bags of a white powder being dealt out. Damn, he knew cocaine when he saw it. That's when he took the jab.

He took his time getting up from the floor as he glanced around, noted another group of three men doing the same, money exchanging hands for cocaine. Damn.

Hunter got up to his feet and managed to get in a couple of good jabs himself against his opponent but then paused and glanced over to his right and saw four men in a corner, all of them shooting up with syringes. Heroine, he guessed. One of the men was the house guard. The other guard, the one he guessed was the informant was nowhere in sight.

Holding off Connor with a couple more quick jabs he looked around for the pastor. He wasn't in the gym. Damn, he wondered where he was since he didn't want Regina's escape plan possibly being circumvented by the pastor.

Hunter came to a dead halt, wished he had his damned phone with him but had left it in their suite.

Damn, he and Regina had fallen into a drug ring, a fairly large one when he counted at least twenty men in the gym, all either shooting up or snorting, buying and selling between each other.

"Hey, old man!" a voice shouted at him. "Had enough?"

Hunter turned just in time to take a direct hit in the cheekbone and darkness fell over him as he crumpled to the floor.

CHAPTER TWENTY-ONE

Regina, dressed in skinny jeans, t-shirt and hoodie, left her suite; Hunter had left the door unlocked so she headed down the hallway for her quarry. Saving Matilda was the only thing on her mind.

She went down the hallway, to the very end, turned the corner into the next hallway and midway down reached Matilda's suite. Looking surreptitiously around her, she was satisfied the hallway was vacant. She tried turning the knob and sighed when it wouldn't budge. But she was prepared. Digging out the pin from her pocket she stuck it in the doorknob hole, jiggled it around and she heard a click, breathing a relieved sigh. Never had she been happier than now for Hunter's directions on how to pick a doorknob lock. And these doorknob lock assembles were not new technology.

She turned the knob, pushed open the door, found Matilda and gasped. The woman had been trussed up on her knees, her face buried in a pillow, handcuffed with her hands behind her, naked. Cringing, Regina saw her ass had recently been whipped for several neat rows of stripes crossed the creamy skin. She squirmed on the bed as Regina closed the door behind her and locked it, then scampered to the poor woman's side.

"Hold still while I figure out if I can pick the lock on the cuffs open," Regina whispered.

Immediately, Matilda stilled.

After a few minutes, Regina cursed. "Damn, this pin isn't working on these." Hearing muffled words from Matilda, who had also been gagged, she reached up and removed what appeared to be her scrunched up underwear from her mouth.

"The keys, he has them," she whispered.

Cursing beneath her breath, Regina looked around, murmuring, "There has to be a way…"

"No, there isn't a way, Mrs. Monroe. Lie down on the bed, next to Ms. Matthews."

Regina's head jerked up and she glared at the pastor who stood in the doorway, his big, pudgy body imposing, taking up the entire space. She decided, in that moment, she could take him. Rising from the bed she took a couple steps toward him but came to an abrupt halt when he reached into his back waistband and pulled out a gun—a small Smith and Wesson. She might be able to rush him before he could get a shot off she decided and before she could run more than three steps he shot her in the shoulder.

She gasped, started to go down but stood several feet away from him, holding her shoulder as blood started trickling down her body, through her hoodie. Glancing down, she saw red and gasped. She'd never been shot before, even in the line of duty, so she was stunned by the pain arcing through her upper body from just one bullet.

"One more step and I'll shoot again, only in a more deadly location. Now get on the bed."

Regina knew she had no choice and she stumbled around the bed and laid down on her back beside Matilda who was openly sobbing now.

"On your stomach, Mrs. Monroe."

She gasped as she slowly rolled over at the pain from having to put weight on the injured shoulder. She heard his footsteps then, felt him draw near. She heard him breathing next to her now and she looked up at him and saw his leering expression.

"You are a beautiful woman, Mrs. Monroe. It's a shame I had

to shoot you, but I knew you planned on attacking me—even with a gun in my hand. Stupid, very stupid."

"Hunter will kill you for this," she grit out.

"No, your husband has just been in the ring, a fight he provoked between himself and Mr. Johnson, I might add. Johnson knocked him out cold, so don't expect any help from him," he added.

———

Hunter slowly roused, looked bleary-eyed around him and saw he was surrounded by several men. He remembered then, he was in the gym, and had viewed most of the men indulging in drugs. His bleary-eyed expression slowly left then when he noticed their gawking, laughing, sneering faces, knowing they were all high.

"I'll help you up to your place," a man said.

Hunter looked to his right as the man took his arm and helped him to his feet. "You took a hard, direct jab for sure," the man said.

"Tell me something I don't know," Hunter growled. Looking around he saw Connor in a corner, still doing a line and shook his head to clear it. He looked at the man who'd helped him up and recognized the guard whom he assumed was the plant.

"You need help getting back to your place?" the man asked, sounding straight and normal. Yep, had to be the plant.

"No. I can make it. Thanks, though. Who are you?"

The man looked around as he walked him to the corridor. "Agent Sylvester Cromwell."

"From?" Hunter asked.

"DEA. I'll help you out to the corridor to make sure you can make it," he insisted, his gaze riveted on Hunter. Okay, it was obvious the guy wanted to talk to him alone.

At Hunter's nod he allowed the guy to help him. Once in the corridor the guard held his arm and as they walked the guard grumbled.

"What the hell are you doing, man? Who the hell are you?"

"P.I. Hunter Monroe. Here on a mission for a client to retrieve their daughter."

"Who?" he snapped.

"Matilda Matthews."

"Damn good thing," he said, shaking his head. "That poor woman has been in here for weeks as you likely know and she's in rough shape. Her boyfriend, the guy who beat the hell out of you, is a real sadist. She's lucky to be alive."

"Right," Hunter said. "Don't you think they'll think it strange you didn't participate?"

"I did one line right when they broke out the stuff. I'm wearing a wire and I have it all recorded, thanks to the diversion you made in the ring with Connor. I've been trying for weeks to break this ring and it looks like, with your inadvertent help, I did it."

"So this is the first time you've caught them all in the act?"

"Where I could record them, yes. Cause usually the pastor is in here with all of us, which makes me wonder where in the hell he is now. He should have been in the gym, like usual."

"And these guys drag out the drugs even with the pastor here?"

"No, they don't, hence my opportunity this time."

"So do you think the pastor doesn't know about it?"

"Oh, he knows, heard him on a phone call when he didn't realize I was nearby. He's the head of this entire operation. Keeps the lowest profile, though."

They had arrived at Hunter's door. "Why hasn't the pastor invited me into this ring when he obviously invited the others."

"Because all of the others have been a part of this for a long time. The pastor watches and waits for the opportunity to involve certain guys, based on their behavior once they're in here with the wives or girlfriends. Some of the patrons leave after the designated time they signed up for, but the ones that keep signing up over and over again the pastor gets them involved."

"What? They're all addicts?"

"Hell, yes, but also, they get a piece of the pie so to speak from the outside sales they make."

"So they're selling outside the church?" At Cromwell's nod, Hunter asked, "What about the women?"

"They're completely in the dark and believe the pastor's bull-shit about being 'taken in hand'. Blind love is what I say."

"So you got the guys but not the pastor, who will likely deny everything."

Cromwell shrugged. "He might, but I have his phone call recorded—two of them. I was waiting and hoping to find more people involved and now that I have we'll raid the place. Also, his financials might show us even more."

"Sounds like a plan. I need to get my hands on the pastor first before you take him down."

Scowling, Cromwell asked, "Why?"

"Fucker's a creep. What he condones these men do to these women—"

Cromwell held up a hand. "Understood. No qualms from me. Never saw a thing. I'll let you know when I'll be making my move."

Hunter entered his suite and stopped cold. "Regina?" He walked through the living area to the bathroom. The door was wide open and no Regina. "Shit," he snapped as he strode to the door and left the suite, leaving it unlocked in case she returned before him.

He started to make a left at the next hallway but stopped and backed up around the corner. Connor Johnson was at his door, ready to enter.

Damn. He hoped Regina wasn't inside their room.

———

Regina screamed against the gag—her underwear—unable to stop herself. The pastor had trussed her up in the same position as Matilda, having her completely undress before. He stood behind her, laughing merrily as he swung, with a heavy hand, a long wooden crop against her ass. Never had she experienced such excruciating pain as this, even at Hunter's hand.

Again and again he struck her, laughing with maniacal glee.

"You thought you fooled me, didn't you, Mrs. Monroe? Who planted you here? What agency? They've tried before and couldn't prove a thing and they won't now!" he growled.

Dizzy and feeling close to passing out, Regina screamed as loud as she could behind the gag, praying Hunter would find them—soon.

Her knees hurt from being in this prone position, but it was nothing like the pain in her ass. Indescribable, she couldn't imagine any woman wanting this treatment, though Hunter had said some did. What had he called them? Ah yes, pain sluts —masochists.

Tears flooded her eyes; how many times had he struck her? Ten, or more? She'd lost count. She stiffened when she heard the sound of a lock. Someone was here or the pastor had left, she prayed. She starting shaking even harder when she heard another male voice.

"Well, well, Pastor, you've been a busy man, haven't you?"

Connor Johnson had found them and while she should feel ecstatic at this she knew they weren't saved. He'd left Matilda in this position after beating her—what made her think he'd save her?

"What the hell are you doing here?" Pastor Griffin snarled.

"This is my suite, isn't it?"

Regina heard footsteps and slammed her eyes shut, then she fought the gag again, trying to speak around it, until a hand grabbed her ponytail, turned her head and she met Connor's snide expression.

"Ah, Mrs. Monroe, of course. I had a feeling you and your husband were snooping around in other peoples' business. You certainly didn't behave like a surrendered wife to my expectations."

Glaring at him, she struggled against the handcuffs cuffing her wrists behind her back to no avail.

"Pastor, retrieve that frat paddle of mine. It's in the closet," Connor drawled. Then Regina heard him say, "What the hell? Why is she bleeding, Pastor?"

"Shot her."

"You what—why?"

"She was coming at me and—"

"You shot her? Are you insane?" Connor shouted. "You're the one giving us advice on controlling a woman and you had to use a gun on her?" he growled. "Damn it, man, what do you think she'll do once she leaves this place? She'll snitch on us!"

"We'll deal with that issue when the time comes," the pastor snarled.

Within moments, Regina started crying in earnest for she felt wood rubbing against her ass. Obviously, her being shot wasn't going to stop Connor from beating her. She twisted her hands trying to free herself, but she was caught tight. Then she nearly swallowed her tongue when 'splat', searing pain tore through her hind quarters.

"A few more I think so she gets the message, don't you think, Pastor?"

"Absolutely," the pastor replied.

Regina heard the sound of air moving and she knew he'd swung the paddle back, ready to let it fly at her again when pounding then the sound of breaking wood met her ears.

A roar sounded in the suite then and she slumped in relief at the sound of Hunter's shouts and swearing. She could barely turn toward the noise of a fist punching someone followed by more grunts and groans. And then nothing but the sweet oblivion of darkness encompassed her.

.

CHAPTER TWENTY-TWO

Brilliant light shone in her eyes and she cried out, "Stop, that light is killing me!"

"Just checking your eyes, Officer Arrigoni," a soft woman's voice said. "Sorry."

Regina opened her eyes carefully and looked into a pair of dark brown eyes very close to her face, holding a small light.

"Good. You're coming out of the anesthesia now. You had us a bit worried," the woman said.

Regina glanced around and found only this woman in the room.

"To your unsaid question, I'm Dr. Ralston, and you are in the hospital. Do you remember anything?"

Groaning, Regina tried scooting up in the bed but gasped at the pain tearing through her body. "Do I remember? Damned right, I do. How long have I been here?"

"You were brought in late afternoon. It's now midnight. You had surgery to remove a bullet from your shoulder and are just coming out of anesthesia."

"Oh, yes, I was shot," Regina replied. Looking around frantically, she added, "Where is Hunter?"

"Who?" the doctor asked, confused.

"The man I was with."

The doctor shook her head. "Sorry, you were brought in by ambulance, by yourself."

Regina's heart broke at the thought Hunter hadn't thought enough to come to the hospital with her, and when she'd spent two days with him two years ago when he'd been shot.

"I see, well, thank you."

"We did manage to find your parents and they have been notified and are on their way."

"Coming from Florida then," Regina murmured.

"Yes, they should be here any time," the woman said reassuringly.

Just then the door to her room opened and a man and a woman in their late forties came rushing in.

"Oh, honey," her mother, Maria Arrigoni sobbed. "Are you all right?"

Her father, Joseph Arrigoni, came in right behind her and rushed to the opposite side of the bed. "We've been worried about you, kitten," her father said, moving Regina to tears.

"Watch her shoulder," Dr. Ralston warned.

She needed her mom and dad right now and didn't care if they hurt her with their hugs. They each hugged her, careful of her bound up shoulder.

Her mother looked beautiful, as usual. Regina always felt like an ugly duckling around her mother—her beauty not just on the surface but skin deep. She wore her long, wavy, tawny colored hair up in a messy bun, her frame was tall and lean—Regina had inherited her height but not the lean part, unfortunately.

Sniffling, she said, "It's good to see you, Mom." She looked at her handsome, dark-haired dad with a slightly brawny build—she took after him more than Mom. "And you too, Dad. Thanks for coming."

"Thanks for coming? Hell, you wouldn't be able to keep us away!" Taking a seat in a vacant chair next to the bed, he added, "You want to talk about it?"

Regina immediately shook her head. "No, not now…not yet. Not ready," she said.

They made small talk for a while until Regina said, "I think I do want to talk about it a bit."

"Whatever you want," her mom said.

———

Hunter got off the elevator and made his way swiftly to the nurse station. Leaning toward a pretty blonde-haired nurse, he asked, "Regina Arrigoni's room?"

She gave him a brilliant grin, sweeping her eyes over him. "Are you a relative of the patient?"

"No. Co-worker. We're cops—together."

"I will need to see some I.D. as I have a list of approved visitors."

He dug out his wallet from his inside jacket pocket and whipped out his I.D.

"All right," she said, scanning the short list. "You're on it. Room 627, just down to your right, last door, left side."

Without a word, he tore down the hallway and when he reached her room noticed the door was open. He started to enter but paused at the sound of Regina talking. After listening a few minutes, he realized these were her parents. He'd met them a few times when he and Regina worked together, so he knew of them. He took another step forward but paused again.

"I love him, Mom."

Her dad's gruff voice sounded. "You must since you got shot working with him. Where in the hell was he at that damned place? He should have backed you up—shouldn't have left you alone."

"It's not his fault, Dad," Regina said, then groaned as she tried sitting up higher in the bed.

Hunter stayed in place as guilt plagued him. He should make his presence known, and her father was right; he should have kept her in his sites and not left her alone a second while they had been at that damned house.

"It's not like the two of you didn't know each other—hell, you'd worked together for two years!" her father snapped.

"Dear, enough," Regina's soft voice floated to Hunter's ears. "It's done. Hunter did the best he could, I'm sure."

Thank you, Mrs. Arrigoni.

"Where is Monroe anyway?" her dad asked irritably.

Hunter straightened his shoulders and chose that moment to saunter into Regina's room. His hands were shoved into the pockets of his leather jacket as he moved toward Regina, his gaze raking over her from head to toe. Even shot, and in a hospital gown, she was beautiful.

"Hunter!" Regina exclaimed then a smile wreathed her face.

Feeling more confident about his appearance he smiled in return and paused at the opposite side of her bed from her parents. Leaning down he kissed her forehead and his grin widened when he couldn't straighten as she'd grabbed hold of his jacket lapel.

"Thank God you're all right," she whispered.

"You too," he said as he clasped one of her hands in his and she released her hold on his jacket. He raised his eyes to her father. "And you were right, Mr. Arrigoni. I should have kept her with me the entire time I was there. In hindsight, I shouldn't have left her in the room alone."

Mr. Arrigoni narrowed his eyes on him, taking in his words before nodding.

"Lesson learned," the older man growled.

Hunter looked at Regina again. "When are they letting you out of here?"

"I'm hoping tomorrow though the doctor hasn't said yet."

"Oh, sweetheart, that's too soon," her mother said.

"I agree with your mom, Regina," Hunter said. "A few more days can only help with the healing." Grimacing, he asked, "Are you in a lot of pain?"

"No," Regina replied, but then she looked at the bags of liquid hooked up to her, "but I'm sure there's plenty of pain relievers in those bags."

"Good thing too," Hunter said. "No worries, though, once you go home I'll be moving in to care for you until you're completely healed."

Regina's eyes widened. "You can't do that!" she protested. "What about your business?"

Hunter shrugged. "I'm owed some time off so stop worrying."

"That won't be necessary, Monroe," Mr. Arrigoni said. "We cancelled our Caribbean cruise and plan on taking care of Regina once she goes home. We'll be there for as long as she needs us."

"Oh, no," Regina groaned. "You have been planning that trip for a year. You guys go. I'll be fine," she added.

"We already rescheduled the trip for next spring, her mother said. "No worries, dear."

———

Regina caught the twinkle in her mom's eyes and narrowed her gaze on her. Were they trying to keep herself and Hunter apart? She knew they'd always liked him so she couldn't see why they were doing this. She imagined it was her dad who planned this since he blamed Hunter for her injury, but it wasn't Hunter's fault.

"Truly, I insist you go."

"Not a chance," her father said. He looked at Hunter. "You're welcome to swing by and visit but we'll be staying with Regina at her house for as long as she needs our help."

"Of course, sir," Hunter murmured.

While Regina appreciated her parents offer of help once she left the hospital, she'd much rather it was Hunter. But he'd caved into her father—not surprising since Hunter had always been reasonable, responsible, and a gentleman. Sighing, she turned away from the three people who meant so much to her and closed her eyes as exhaustion enveloped her.

———

A week later found Regina situated on the sofa in her living room with her parents hovering over her. And all she could think was how would she put up with these two for the next month? Not only did they hover but they rarely left her alone. Even while sleeping she sensed their presence in the room. And when she'd awaken from resting they'd ply her with food and drink. They'd help her in and out of the bathroom, too. She'd put her foot down firmly though when her mother suggested she go in and help her.

Two more weeks passed, and it was early November and Illinois had had its first major snowstorm of the season. As Regina looked out her living room windows a low feeling overwhelmed her. She appreciated her parents' help but wanted to see Hunter —needed to see him. He hadn't called her or visited since she left the hospital. She knew he was likely busy with work, but she was worried; she'd called him, and his phone always went to voice mail. She'd left a few messages, but he never returned her call.

Thanksgiving was in two weeks, and she planned on inviting him to her house for dinner but then decided against it. He had a family she was sure he'd spend the holidays with—as did she. Guilt encompassed her though as she found herself wishing her parents would leave her and return home, but the month wasn't up yet. And they had promised her a month's stay.

In her recliner she sat, checking email on her iPad when she heard a sound—was that a car door slamming? She started to rise from her chair when her mother entered the living room.

"Stay there, sweetheart. Your father is getting the door. It appears you have company. Isn't that nice?" she asked with a brilliant smile.

Regina sank back and frowned, wondering who would be visiting her? She heard voices then and looking over her shoulder she smiled when Chief Maria Sanchez entered the living room. Her boss was dressed in one of her royal blue skirt suits, looking capable as well as beautiful as usual.

"Chief Sanchez! Oh, let me get up and get you—"

"Stay put, Regina. I just came by to check and see how you're doing," she said with a glance over her shoulder. "I can see you've got lots of help, a good thing for you in the healing process." Her smile slipped. "How are you doing? I know what it's like to take a bullet."

"Have a seat," Regina encouraged her, delighted to have

someone else to talk to aside from her parents. "I'm doing fine, and I feel like I'm about ready to return to work when you'll have me back."

The chief bit her lip and said hesitantly, "About that—"

"What?" Regina asked slowly. "I am ready, seriously."

Chief Sanchez sighed. "I—I had to replace your assigned patrol post."

Nodding, Regina replied, "Oh, that's all right because remember you promised me the next vacant detective job."

"I—did—for sure, and it will be yours once we get over our current budget problems."

"Budget problems?" Regina said, deadpanned.

"City council met and decided they needed to tighten the belts on our upcoming funding, decreasing our promised amount equivalent to one officer salary."

"So I don't have a job?" Regina whispered.

"I'm sorry, I really am, but we can't hire one more detective for the next eighteen months."

"What! But I have a house payment, and bills and—oh, my god, I should never have taken the job with Hunter!" she protested.

"Yes, you should have, you did, and you proved yourself and earned that promotion. I'm not done working with the council on the possibility of getting that promotion for you in the next year, but until then my hands are truly tied."

Chief Sanchez rose from her seat, walked over to Regina and gave her a short hug. "Things will work out, you'll see. Just hang in there for a bit longer," she encouraged her. "You know I have a lot of clout with city hall. I just have to convince them how important it is to hire another detective for our city." She picked up her coat and donned it again. "By the way, have you heard from Monroe since you came home from the hospital?"

"Not a word," Regina said, shaking her head. "It's like he fell off the face of the world."

The chief gave her an encouraging smile. "I'm sure he'll be in touch shortly."

Shell-shocked was what Regina felt as the chief left her house, then her parents trailed in. Her father sat down on the coffee table facing her, took her hands in his.

"You know, you could always sell this place and move in with us."

Gulping back tears, Regina shook her head. "I love my house. I am not selling it, but thanks, Dad, for the offer. I'll figure something else out." She was deep in thought and didn't notice her father leave the living room.

Later that evening, as she sat reading news online she gasped at an article. It was a story about Matilda Matthews and the House of Christian Love. The place had been shut down because there was found to be a huge drug ring stemming from the place. The pastor was in jail. Many of the women who'd been at the house had been there against their will, aside from Matilda, and had filed civil suits against the house. Matilda and the other women were safe and back with their families.

Scowling, she read the rather lengthy article and slammed her iPad lid shut when there was no mention of her being a part of closing down the ring; everything in the article had been about Monroe. Every word was about how he'd bravely entered the facility with no weapon and managed to arrest all involved in the drug scheme and close down the house.

Her mother bustled in then with the mail and placed it on the coffee table. "Daily mail," she said cheerily.

"Thanks, Mom," came Regina's grumpy reply.

Idly, she picked up an envelope from one of her credit card companies and sighed. So much for paying these babies off—that gave her pause. Hunter owed her that money yet to pay off her credit cards. She'd done the job, they'd succeeded, he'd gotten all the accolades so the least he could do was pay off her damned bills.

She opened the statement and gasped at the zero amount, then grinned like she hadn't since seeing him in the hospital. He'd come through and had paid it off. The entire amount. Joy settled inside her, then slowly ebbed away. But why wouldn't he call her or return her calls?

In the next week, Regina discovered not only had Hunter

paid off her credit cards but also the $85,000 left on her mortgage. She tried calling him but got the answering machine again. Again, she left messages.

Thanksgiving arrived and Regina and her mom prepared a traditional dinner. Regina was feeling so much better and ate more than she had in a long while. By 4:00 p.m., bellies stuffed, while Regina helped her mother put away leftovers she heard the front doorbell ring.

"I'll get it!" she heard her father call out from where he sat in the living room, watching a football game.

"I'd better go see who it is," Regina said.

"Oh, let your father handle it, sweetheart. He'll let us know in a minute I'm sure."

Narrowing her eyes on her mom she said, "What's going on? Why don't you want me going to the door?"

A low, baritone voice said, "Because you might learn that I've been trying to get a hold of you for weeks."

Regina whirled around to see Hunter standing in the kitchen doorway. She ran to him, threw her arms around his neck with a sob.

"I—I thought you'd forgotten about me," she murmured, feelings tears in her eyes and a tightness in her chest as he buried her head against his shoulder.

He hugged her close. "Never would I forget you." He stepped back and looked deeply into her eyes. "Why didn't you answer your phone when I returned your calls, though?"

Frowning, she said, "Because you never did return my calls."

"I did, several times, but either your father answered the phone, or it would roll over immediately to your voice mail."

"Joseph!" her mom gasped.

CHAPTER TWENTY-THREE

"Dad!" Regina exploded. "You know I've been waiting for Hunter to call. What did you do?"

Sheepishly, he said, "I did a bit of tampering with your phone is all." Then, sticking his broad chest out, added, "Thought you needed complete rest while you healed and didn't need to be talking to Monroe during this time so I silenced your phone."

"I didn't think to check the ringer, assuming it was on. You had no right," Regina scolded. "How could you?"

"I think he was simply doing what a father believes is best for his child," Hunter said.

Her dad nodded briskly. "Absolutely."

"So you're saying you weren't trying to keep us apart?" she inquired.

"Hell, no!" he shouted. "Why would I do that?"

"Because you blame Hunter for my being hurt, that's why, and you know damned well it isn't his fault. You and mom can leave—anytime now."

"Oh, sweetheart," her mom said, "we just wanted to help."

"You did, but as you can see I'm perfectly well now. See if you can reschedule that trip to leave earlier than spring."

Her mom looked at her dad. "Maybe we can reschedule it for right after Christmas?"

Regina caught the hopeful tone in her mom's voice and smiled. "Perfect idea. Now why don't the two of you get packed, call the airlines and see if you can book a flight back home tomorrow. I'll call a cab to pick you up once you let me know the time."

"That sounds perfect, Regina," her mom said, taking her husband by the elbow and leading him out of the kitchen and down the hall to their room to pack, scolding him in sharp whispers.

"But wait, Maria, we can't just leave—

"We've more than outstayed our welcome, Joseph, so come along," Regina heard her mom say.

Once they left the room, Regina looked at Hunter, leaning against the doorframe, his gaze hot and heavy on her.

"I'm hoping you're staying overnight?" Regina asked.

"Got a bag in the car."

"What about Thanksgiving with your family?"

"We had an early brunch at the Langham Hotel restaurant, per my mom needing a holiday off from cooking. Worked for me because here I am before nightfall." He lifted his arms away from his body, offering himself to her and she grinned, stepping into his embrace once more.

"You saved me you know."

He sighed. "No, I didn't. You were shot. I didn't make it back to that room in time."

"I meant from another day with my parents hovering over me!"

"So how do you think they'll handle it when you marry me?"

She gasped and stepped back. "You want to get married?"

"Right now if I could, but I've a feeling your parents wouldn't allow it." With that he sank to one knee and pulled a small black box from his pocket.

"In a way, I'm glad your dad gave us time to think about things when we were apart. It put in complete perspective for me what I want in life. My first marriage was a disaster, no two ways about it, but this one, with you, won't be, I'm sure of it. We gel, Regina, me and you." He pulled an emerald cut diamond engagement ring from the box and said, "Will you marry me?"

"In a heartbeat," she said softly as she sank down to the floor facing him.

He placed the ring on her finger, then took her carefully into his arms once more. "You do know that me being a dominant doesn't prevent you from having a say in our marriage, don't you? But final decisions will be made by me."

She frowned as she moved back from his arms. "What do you mean?"

With a sigh, he said, "I allowed Sheila to control much of what happened in our marriage. I was busy, working all kinds of crazy hours as a cop, and didn't spend the time I needed with her to make sure things were okay—that she was happy. I don't plan on that happening again. Owning my own business allows me the choice and opportunity to spend a lot of time with you, which I plan on doing. I'm a dominant but that doesn't mean I won't allow you to have opinions, and to consider them when we make decisions about things in our marriage. We will always have choices to make—together. And hopefully those choices will be satisfactory to us both. Do you understand what I'm saying?"

"Yes, I do. You are the man I've wanted my entire life, Hunter. I value you and your opinions and trust you to know what's best for us in our marriage. But I don't ever want to be treated the way those women at the house were—it's not in me to cave that way."

"And I wouldn't want you to be like that, either. But know that 'vanilla' isn't really me, either. I will have expectations of you, in our bedroom, and at the club, if you choose to go with me there."

Her eyes widened. "You plan on keeping your membership at the K Club?"

"Yes but know that I won't ever force you to go there with me."

She nodded. "But does that mean if I don't want to go to the club, you won't go, either?"

"That's right. I won't go there if you're not with me."

With a sly grin, Regina said, "Well, maybe I'll let you buy a multi-utility bench for our bedroom then. We won't ever have to go to the club if we have one of those, right?"

"We won't need it. The bed works just fine for all kinds of activities, besides sleeping," he said with a laugh.

Frowning, she asked, "Where will we live? Your place or mine?"

"Chief Sanchez called and told me she can't hire you on right away as a detective so I was thinking maybe you could move into my place and help me with my business. If you don't want to sell your house then we could rent it out until we decide for sure where we want to live. I can run my business from anywhere."

She widened her eyes on him. "Oh! I could be a P.I. too then! At least until I can get hired on as a detective."

"Um, I was thinking more of helping me out with the office stuff—to help me run the business, not as an investigator."

"Hunterrrr," she groaned. "You know how much I hate desk work."

He sighed. "I figured that wouldn't fly with you."

"No. I'm a cop and a good one, you can't deny that."

"No, I can't deny it, but I want you safe. Now that I'll be your husband, your safety will always be important to me."

"And I feel the same way about you."

Hesitantly, he said, "We'll give it a try, the two of us working some cases together and see how it pans out."

"Yes!" she said gleefully. "I knew you'd see it my way."

"I said we'd give it a try," he warned.

"O-kay," she said, biting her lip.

He scowled at her and shook at finger at her. "You will listen to me, follow all directions from me when we work a case. Got it? It'll be no different than when we were partners as cops."

She saluted him as she rose to her feet. "Absolutely," she said, tucking her hands behind her back and crossing her fingers.

"I'm not fooling around, Regina," he growled.

She heard her parents walking down the hall, arguing, thinking how they sounded an awful lot like them. She took Hunter's hand. "Let's inform my parents we're getting married."

He pulled back and jammed his hands on his hips. "I want your promise, Regina, you will follow all of my directions, or you'll be behind the desk you hate."

"Sounds perfect to me," her dad said with a nod.

"Dad," Regina whined.

"You know I've always hated you being a cop," he retorted. "A desk job makes sense to me."

"I don't need two fathers, you know." She scowled between the two of them.

Hunter turned to her dad and stuck out his hand. "I think we finally found something to agree on."

Her father took his hand. "Deal."

THE END

———

Don't miss out on your next favorite book!

Join the Satin Romance mailing list
www.satinromance.com/mail.html